Murder in the Cultural Gardens

Dan Hanson

No part of this book may be reproduced or transmitted in any form or by any means, electronic or mechanical, including photocopying, recording, or by any information and storage retrieval system without the written permission of the publisher.

This book is a work of fiction. Names, characters, places and incidents are either a products of the author's imagination or are used fictitiously. Any resemblance to actual events, locales or persons, living or dead, is entirely coincidental.

Dan Hanson, Publisher
868 Montford Rd.
Cleveland Heights, OH 44121
http://www.murderintheculturalgardens.com/

Library of Congress Control Number: 2019911120.

ISBN-13: 978-1-7125-2956-0

DEDICATION

To my father Norm Hanson as promised and
my mother Pat Hanson who made it all possible.

ACKNOWLEDGMENTS

Thanks to the board members and staff of the Cleveland Cultural Gardens Federation and One World Day team including President Wael Khoury M.D., Past-Presidents Sheila Crawford and Paul Burik, Connie Adams, Thomas Turkaly, Sam Tanious, Paula Tilisky, Lori Ashyk, Pierre Bejjani, Yvonne Conwell, Carl Ewing, Mehmet Gencer, Qaisra Haider, Dan Hanson, George Terbrak, Debbie Hanson, Dozia Krislaty, Erika Puussaar, Svetlana Stolyarova, Johnny Wu, Angela Woodson, Asim Datta, Anda Cook, Oanh Loi-Powell and Laura Tershko.

CHAPTER 1

It just didn't seem right to DJ. A body found bludgeoned to death in a place known for "Peace through Mutual Understanding." But there she was, crumpled behind a tribute to composer Franz Liszt in the Hungarian Cultural Garden.

He pulled out his cell phone and dialed 911. "What is the nature of your emergency?" the dispatcher queried. With a suddenly very dry mouth DJ managed to get out, "There's been a murder in the Cultural Gardens."

CHAPTER 2

It had started like most weekend mornings that summer. Dick "DJ" Jamieson and his friends and colleagues Ren Wu and Peggy Powell were in the Cleveland Cultural Gardens working on a project that they hoped would put their startup company on the map – and bring in some much-needed income. The trio had a variety of complementary skills and after years of using those skills for various volunteer projects around Cleveland they decided to start their own company.

Dick Jamieson had been called DJ since he was born. He was 6'2 with jet black hair and a square jawline. He seemed to always have a five-o'clock shadow. His powerful physique harkened back to what he called his "jock days" in high school and college. A seeming oxymoron, DJ's athletic prowess did not interfere with his logical mind that pursued physics, math and, of course, technology.

His best friend Ren Wu was a combination of martial artist, gadget guru and film producer. His willingness to take chances to get just the right shot earned him the nickname Reckless Ren. He was of Chinese heritage and looked the part, resembling a young Bruce Lee. Fluent in several languages, Ren enjoyed when people guessed his first language to be Chinese. It was actually Spanish because he was born in Panama to diplomat parents. If there was a new gadget released, Ren would be all over it. His fan and feature films were beginning to garner national attention.

Peggy Powell was a nature buff and artist who could identify variations of plants from 50 feet away. She didn't have the tech chops of DJ or Ren but she brought a different perspective, and an artist's eye, to their projects. She had long brown hair and green eyes that popped out from her collection of oversized glasses. She was as introverted as Ren was outgoing and often hid her face behind her long locks parted in the middle. The guys had fun making her blush and treated her like a kid sister.

The three had met while volunteering on several different projects and soon saw that their complimentary skills made them a productive team. After a few trial runs they decided to formalize their relationship and start a business.

Theirs was a classic case of working "in" the business instead of "on" it and income was scarce. So when they met a Cleveland University professor who offered to back a summer long project they jumped at the chance. And with the subject of the project being one of their favorite places, the Cleveland Cultural Gardens, they were ecstatic. Little did they know the joy would not last as the project would lead them into a web of danger and murder.

CHAPTER 3

The Cultural Gardens are a 250 acre plot of land on Cleveland's east side that was donated by John D. Rockefeller to the city over 100 years ago. Yes, that John D. Rockefeller.

In 1916 a Shakespeare enthusiast named Leo Weidenthal tailored a spot in the park to honor the Bard and called it the Shakespeare Garden. Gateposts at the entrance are of English design and visitors can follow a path flanked by hedges to a bust of Shakespeare in the rear of the garden.

The flora includes a mulberry tree grown from a cutting from the tree that Shakespeare himself planted back in Stratford. Other trees were planted by famous Shakespeare actors and by Irish poet and Nobel Prize winner William Butler Yeats. It is claimed that Rabindranath Tagore–the "Shakespeare of India"– and the actress Sarah Bernhardt also planted flowers.

But the bust of Shakespeare is the main feature of the Garden along with a plaque and Royal Oak dedicated by the Queen herself. It eventually became the British Garden and evolved into a celebration of British culture more than just a Shakespeare tribute.

Ten years later another plot was carved out – this time celebrating Jewish culture in what was called the Hebrew Garden. Weidenthal had a vision to turn the 250-acre park into a special place celebrating the dozens of different ethnic groups and cultures that had come to Cleveland over the years.

That vision came true and soon there were cultural gardens for Irish, Italian, German, Polish and other heritages. Statues and busts honoring cultural heroes were created. Special landscaping, including trees and flowers from the particular country, were added. Events celebrating ethnic heritage were held.

As the population of Cleveland grew more diverse, the Cultural Gardens added new heritages reflecting those changes. African-American, Chinese, Serbian, Croatian, Syrian, Turkish and other gardens were established. Over 30 cultures are represented with another 15 or so in the works.

DJ, Ren and Peggy were longtime fans of the Gardens and had spent countless hours taking photos and video of the unique-in-the-world location. They volunteered for Garden events such as the annual One World Day, Opera in the Italian Garden and others. One day they met Cleveland College professor Dr. Trebor Raselok in the Syrian Garden and they struck up a conversation.

Raselok was about 60 years old and had salt and pepper hair that kept falling into his eyes. He was about 6'5" but walked with a slight stoop that suggested he had sat hunched over his desk for years. Raselok was in the Gardens that day researching the Syrian poet Nizar Quabbani. He was taking some photos of a bust of the poet with what gadget guru Ren laughingly called "a toy camera."

The professor told them of his plan to produce a multimedia project about the Cultural Gardens. He wanted to show the rest of the world this impressive tribute to "Peace through Mutual Understanding" which was the motto of the Cleveland Cultural Gardens Federation, the organization whose volunteers maintained and grew the Gardens.

As they listened, the three looked at each other excitedly and then pitched the professor their services. Raselok jumped at the chance to have a passionate, talented crew make his dream a reality and the three jumped at the chance to work on a project they loved – and actually get paid! Plus, this would be a nice addition to their portfolio to show prospective clients.

The project was going great until that morning when everything changed.

CHAPTER 4

Since their contract with Dr. Raselok, the trio visited the Cultural Gardens almost every morning bright and early and got to work. DJ took photos, Ren shot video and Peggy captured the distinctive flora and landmarks of the Gardens in illustrations.

The three met that fateful morning in front of the upper level of the Hungarian Garden on East Blvd. DJ had bought two coffees and one green concoction that Peggy always drank. She was the only one who ever ordered the healthy but foul smelling concoction so the Cultural Garden Coffee Shop down the street had named it the "Peggy." It was guaranteed to redden Peggy's cheeks when she heard someone order a "Peggy".

The morning was already fairly warm but cloudy. That was good. Bright sun could wreak havoc on the high quality photos and videos that they needed to capture. After the usual friendly insults and a critique of the latest Dr. Who episode the three went to work.

Peggy made a side trip to the Turkish Garden to check on the tulips. The window of opportunity to capture them at the peak of their blooms was small and she didn't want to miss it. DJ and Ren were surprised when Peggy told them that though many think of the Dutch when they discuss tulips, tulips are actually native to Turkey.

She told them, "Tulips are the national flower of the Republic of Turkey with a history going back to its Ottoman roots." DJ and Ren recognized that Peggy had that look in her eyes. When she was really into something her green eyes glazed under her large spectacles and she spewed facts like a living Wikipedia.

"Did you know," she offered, "that many cultivated varieties of tulips were widely grown in Turkey long before they were brought to Holland from Turkey in the 16th Century?"

"Did you know," she continued, "the botanical name for tulips, Tulipa, is derived from the Turkish word "tulbend" or "turban", which the flower resembles? It's considered to be the King of Bulbs."

Before she could eject another factoid, Ren interrupted her. "OK, OK, we believe you. Tulips were Turkish first."

"You really surprise us sometimes Peggy," DJ said. "Where do you get this stuff?" Her eyes unglazed, she smiled and replied "I know a lot more than you geeks give me credit for." And she was off down the street toward the Turkish Garden.

Ren set up two video cameras on tripods in different sections of the Hungarian Garden to capture some b-roll shots. He launched his drone with the HD camera and set up his gimbal and other cameras and headed for the southeast corner of the garden.

DJ started setting up his gear and relished the peace and quiet of the space. Unless there was an event, the Gardens were a good place for solitude and quiet and even more so early in the morning.

So when DJ felt a tap on his shoulder he almost jumped out of his skin.

CHAPTER 5

It was Angel Annie. "Sorry to scare you Deej," she apologized. "I just wanted to say 'hi.'" The homeless woman had been part of the Cultural Gardens space since DJ had accidentally "discovered" the park on a bike ride years earlier. Nobody knew much about her. She carried several shopping bags loaded with what looked like junk. They had learned her name was Annie and years ago someone had christened her Angel Annie for her kind nature. It fit.

Her hair was disheveled and she wore several layers of clothing, even on this warm morning. Her cheeks sported some dirt but you could tell that she had at one time been quite good looking. The three had differing opinions on her age but she was probably in her forties or fifties.

It had taken several weeks for Annie to feel safe with DJ, Ren and Peggy (what bad things had happened to her in her past?) and they had become good friends.

Angel Annie didn't just stay in the confines of one or two gardens. She might pop up anywhere in the 250 acres. One of the bags she carried started off empty and would soon be full as she picked up litter that people had left behind. She would then empty it in a trash receptacle and continue on her rounds. Though a harmless soul, she did admit frustration at those who would deface such a beautiful area with their trash.

"Where have you been this morning so far Annie?" DJ asked. "I spent some time in the Hebrew Garden. It was so peaceful," she answered. As the Hebrew Garden was the second garden to be built it really started the chain of Cultural Gardens when it was dedicated in 1926.

The pink Georgia Eweh marble fountain is the centerpiece of the Hebrew Garden. The bowl sits on seven pillars referred to in the Hebrew holy texts. The entire landscape is in the shape of the Star of David.

Like many of the Gardens the Hebrew Garden suffered some theft, vandalism and neglect over the years but the Jewish Federation of Cleveland took over sponsorship of the Hebrew Cultural Garden and made many improvements. This included some new additions honoring Jewish scientists, authors and other cultural figures such as scientists Albert Einstein, Sigmund Freud and Jonas Salk.

Familiar names like Steven Spielberg, Elie Weisel, Emma Lazarus, David Ben Gurion and Golda Meir were included along with historical figures such as Moses Maimonides (Rambam), Abba Eban and Ahad Ha-Am (Asher Ginsberg).

DJ gave her a hug and went over to his gear. He had learned that Annie had a sweet tooth and he often brought her a hot chocolate from the Cultural Gardens Coffee Shop – with extra marshmallows. Annie gave him another hug and took a big sip. She didn't bother to wipe off her chocolate moustache before going about her cleanup business.

The two were startled as something appeared overhead. It turned out to be Ren's drone buzzing them for fun. DJ looked over and saw Ren doubled over in laughter. Typical Ren. Seeing that Ren was all set up DJ picked up the pace in assembling his own gear. He was checking for where the emerging sun was and how it might affect his shots when he heard the unmistakable piercing blast of a police siren.

CHAPTER 6

DJ jerked his head up in alarm and then waved back as Officer O'Malley cruised by laughing at the startled reaction. "I've got to cut down on the coffee," DJ thought. "I am getting too jumpy."

Pat O'Malley was the Cleveland Police officer who, by his request, patrolled the Cultural Gardens and the neighborhood bordering it. He was making his usual morning rounds and this was not the first time that he had startled one of the trio with a quick blast of his siren. O'Malley loved patrolling the Gardens beat and he told everyone he encountered there that he had danced in the Irish Cultural Garden as a kid. Over the years everyone from local school groups to the world champion Murphy Irish Dancers had performed there.

If you searched for a photo of an Irish police officer you would get a picture of Pat O'Malley. Gray curly hair, a reddish bulb of a nose (but not from drinking – O'Malley was a teetotaler) and sparkling eyes made the officer the annual designee for the Santa Claus role at the precinct's Christmas party. O'Malley admitted that each passing year required fewer pillows to make the Santa suit fit.

DJ, Ren and Peggy were becoming used to seeing their fellow Cultural Gardens early birds that summer. Besides Angel Annie and Officer O'Malley, they always ran into Carl Jefferson working in the African American Garden. He was a proud, no-nonsense Vietnam vet who lived in the neighborhood.

Ernie Balogh was another early morning regular. He was a World

War II vet and passionate about his Eastern European heritage. He was a self-described mutt – a mix of Czech, Slovak and Rusyn on his mother's side and Hungarian on his father's side.

Ernie was vocal about not being happy that the name of the main street of the Gardens had been changed from Liberty Blvd (in honor of WWI veterans) to Martin Luther King Jr. Blvd. It had nothing to do with Dr. King. His family had lost many in that "war to end all wars" and he wanted them remembered. He and Carl had numerous, often heated discussions about this but there was a begrudging respect between them.

There were other regulars who worked in their Gardens every weekend: Paul in the Czech Garden, Lex in the Serbian, Tom in the Croatian, Char in the Irish, Gary in the Polish and so on. The trio had befriended them all and eagerly listened to their stories of "their" Gardens. While the City of Cleveland actually owned the land, the volunteers of the Cleveland Cultural Gardens Federation were the ones who did the work, raised the funds, held the events and so on. Anyone and everyone were welcome but it was "their" garden.

DJ was excited. This was going to be a great project – interesting, fun and lucrative – and with his best friends! Nothing could go wrong.

CHAPTER 7

Despite his two bouts of jumpiness, DJ polished off the last of his coffee and started to shoot close-ups of the busts in the Hungarian Garden. He started with the bust of Endre Ady, the Hungarian writer best known for his love poems. Satisfied with those shots he moved on to the statue of Joseph Remenyi, the famous Hungarian-American writer who had taught at Western Reserve University's Cleveland College.

Next was Imre Madach the Hungarian poet and dramatist best known for his dramatic epic, "The tragedy of man; A dramatic poem in fifteen scenes." He shot the impressive gates, trees from Hungary and central courtyard of the Garden. The work was going well – no people around to obstruct his shots and the lighting was bright enough but not causing problems.

DJ headed over to the final monument in the Hungarian Garden and it was his favorite. Honestly, he had never heard of Ady, Remenyi or Madach before this project but everyone had heard of Franz Liszt. Franz Liszt was a Hungarian virtuoso pianist and composer. Liszt is widely considered to be one of the greatest piano virtuosi of all time, and certainly the most famous of the nineteenth century. Some call him the first Rock Star and everyone has heard of Lisztomania.

In fact, the Hungarian Garden was first dedicated on the 123rd anniversary of the birth of Franz Liszt in 1934.

As DJ approached the Liszt tribute, he noticed what looked like some trash that would have to be moved before he could take the photos. Sigh. Like Angel Annie he wondered how people could leave their garbage in such a beautiful place. As he got closer, it became clear that the pile of trash was actually a person. DJ had run into homeless people and others sleeping in the Gardens before. He hoped this was a friendly guy and would move so he could finish his work and get the Liszt shots.

"Sir? Ma'am?" he offered. Nothing. As he got closer he saw that it was a woman and she didn't look very good. "Miss? Ma'am?" Nothing. He just needed a few shots of the Liszt monument and he would be finished. Why did this woman have to sleep off her excesses right here?

He called her a few more times and then gently nudged her side with the toe of his shoe. The sleeping form turned a little and DJ could see a wet red stain matting down the hair on one side of her head. Uh oh. He knelt down and could not see any signs of life. Choking back nausea, he pulled out his phone and called 911.

.

CHAPTER 8

Within minutes, Officer Pat O'Malley pulled up. "What's going on DJ?" he asked. DJ started blurting out the story, not making a lot of sense. "Slow down!" Officer O'Malley commanded. DJ stopped talking and led the cop to the Liszt monument and pointed at the body.

O'Malley knelt down and looked for signs of life. He realized quickly that the body was a corpse and got up warning DJ to not touch anything. He stood up and his head swiveled around as he took in the scene. Satisfied that there was no further imminent danger to anyone he raced to his car to radio for assistance.

"Don't touch anything? Don't worry." DJ thought. He was feeling sick to his stomach and the last thing he wanted to do was see the body again – let alone touch it. The victim, an African American woman about his own age, was so, so "real." This was so different from the gory scenes he had seen in movies and video games.

DJ was almost in a trance as he slowly backed further away from the body. Suddenly he felt something press into the middle of his back. He heard a sinister voice command, "Stick 'em up."

DJ immediately thrust up his hands. He wondered where Officer O'Malley was. His mind was racing. Was this the end? He was about to plead for his life when he heard guffaws from behind.

He spun around and saw Ren convulsing in laughter. Reckless Ren had come back from the other side of the Hungarian Garden to check his video when he saw DJ with his back to him. He couldn't resist sneaking up behind DJ and pressing the lens of his camera into his back. Typical Ren.

Seeing DJ so upset at a pretty harmless prank, he asked, "Why so serious Deej?" in between muffled laughs.

Just then Officer O'Malley returned from his squad car where he had been calling for backup and gathering crime scene tape. Ren's giggles abruptly stopped when he saw what DJ was pointing at. It looked to be a prop from one of his horror movies. The filmmaker in him reacted "Nice job, whoever. Very realistic." He soon realized that it was actually a real body. A real dead body.

"What happened?" Ren gasped. DJ was still too shocked to be coherent but he started to fill Ren in with some of the details. As he told the story, DJ and Ren moved closer to the body and noticed something in the dead girl's hand. DJ started forward when a loud voice barked "Don't take another step!"

CHAPTER 9

Officer O'Malley screamed at the pair to stay away from the body. "This is a crime scene and you could be corrupting evidence." "But Pat," DJ replied, (the guys knew him well enough to call him Pat) "there's something you have to see." There seemed to be something under the victim's head. "It could be a clue!"

"You watch too many videos," the policeman responded. "This is probably just a tragic but random act of violence. The only 'clues' will be discovered by our Crime Lab and Medical Examiner."

As if on cue, other official cars and vans began pulling up. O'Malley told the guys they should stay clear and that he would interview them later. He went to fill in the new arrivals and Ren and DJ looked at each other, nodded, and quickly shot as many photos and videos of the body and surrounding area as they could. They then moved to the neighboring German Garden where they could watch the action and maybe hear some of the discussion.

DJ and Ren stood in silence under the watchful gaze of the Goethe and Schiller monument, lost in thought.

Goethe and Schiller were world renowned philosophers and writers. In the center of the German Garden is the largest monument in the Cleveland Cultural Gardens chain, called, not surprisingly, the

Goethe-Schiller monument. It's a huge statue on a large base. The bronze statue was dedicated in 1907 up the road a little at Wade Park and then rededicated in 1927 in the German Garden. It was designed by artist Ernst Rietschel and cast in1857 and there are similar statues in Weimar, Germany, San Francisco and Milwaukee.

Goethe and Schiller towered over the rest of the German Garden but there were other busts including one of Father Friedrich Jahn who was the founder of calisthenics exercises and designer of all gymnastic apparatuses of modern day (such as the horse, rings, parallel bars and balance beam.)

Other busts were of Alexander Humboldt who was described as the "last universal scholar in the field of natural sciences" and Heinrich Heine the world-famous poet.

Of course there were tributes to composers Johann Sebastian Bach and Ludwig van Beethoven and a marble fountain dedicated to Friedrich Froebel, founder of the Kindergarten System.

But DJ and Ren were concentrating under the gaze of Goethe and Schiller when they were startled by an accusing voice. "So why did you kill the girl?"

CHAPTER 10

It was Katrina DeSanto, the Cleveland Press reporter. DJ and his friends seemed to always be crossing paths with her. They assumed that she didn't like them because their blogs, vlogs and social media postings were more timely, and becoming more popular, than her daily print publication would ever be again.

"We didn't kill her Katrina and you know it," DJ replied. "And what are you doing here anyway?" "I heard the call on my police scanner," she replied. "I should have known that you would be involved. Where's your third wheel?" As if on cue, Peggy raced up and asked, "What's going on?" She had heard the sirens and made her way up the hill as fast as she could.

DJ was about to fill her in when he saw the eager face of the reporter and said "Over here Peggy. I don't want everyone to hear this." The reporter glowered and headed over to the edge of the area that was now cordoned off with crime scene tape.

DJ filled Peggy in and her face turned white. "How awful," she sobbed. "And here of all places - the Cultural Gardens are such a peaceful place."

They watched in silence as the police and crime crew processed the scene. A large scowling man was talking to Officer O'Malley and he pointed their way. "Uh oh," Ren noted. "I don't like the look of that."

Officer O'Malley marched over and said "You three can leave now but we want to interview you DJ at the station later. So don't leave town." "Oooh, I never met a murder suspect before," Ren joked. "Not so fast Ren. The Captain wants you and Peggy to come in too." "Not so funny now, huh Ren?" DJ replied, still shaken from the whole experience. "Let's get out of here."

As they headed back to their cars lugging their gear DJ had a thought. "Depending on when this happened," he offered, "We may have a photo of the murderer!"

The three friends headed back to Ren's studio that served as their office to look at what they had shot that morning. Their downloading and previewing was interrupted by the ringing of DJ's cell phone. It was Officer O'Malley telling DJ to come down to the station for questioning.

"Do you want the others too?" DJ asked. "Not yet," O'Malley answered. "Just you." DJ gulped and headed out leaving Peggy and Ren to work on the image processing. Peggy called out to him "Remember you have the right to an attorney." Ren burst into laughter and added "Don't drop the soap in the shower!" DJ was not amused.

At the station, DJ was ushered into a small uncomfortable room. The door opened and instead of the friendly face of Officer O'Malley he gazed upon the stern, and frightening, countenance of Police Captain Dan Davenport. Davenport was a no-nonsense, rigid cop who would prefer that people would stay out of the Cultural Gardens and other parks. They just caused problems, he always stated.

Davenport paced for a few minutes and then told DJ to tell him everything that had happened that morning. He rattled off question after question.

"What were you doing there?
Did you see it happen?
Did you see anyone else?
Did you hear anything?
Do you know the victim?
Did you touch anything?"

And so on. He grilled DJ on any possible discrepancy or omission. DJ felt like he was the main suspect and that Captain Davenport would be slapping the cuffs on him at any minute. He wondered if Peggy's joke about an attorney might prove to be a reality. Could they really think he had something to do with this?

He looked sideways at Officer O'Malley who tried to look reassuring. But it didn't work. DJ could tell there was something else about to happen.

After what seemed like an eternity of grilling, Captain Davenport pulled out a clear sealed bag with what looked to be a napkin in it. The napkin was imprinted with the logo of the Cultural Gardens Coffee Shop that was on the edge of the Gardens. DJ had seen, and used, dozens of them.

"Is this yours?" the Captain demanded. DJ was stymied. All he saw was a coffee shop napkin. One like thousands of others that were used at the Cultural Gardens Coffee Shop. "How would I know?" he responded. "It's just a napkin. I told you already that I picked up coffee and a Peggy at the Coffee Shop this morning and of course I grabbed a few napkins. Oh, and a hot chocolate for Angel Annie."

"A Peggy?" the Captain prodded. DJ explained the healthy drink his friend always ordered. "Really? So that's your story?" the Captain pressed on. "My story? I have no idea what you are talking about Captain," DJ declared. Captain Davenport snorted with disgust and left the room.

DJ sat there alone and bewildered. What's the big deal with a stupid napkin, he thought. He was about to ask Officer O'Malley when another officer entered the room and told DJ he could leave. The new officer told DJ that he should remain available for further questioning as needed.

"What's going on, Pat?" he asked as they walked out to his car. Officer O'Malley shook his head. "I am not at liberty to say," he answered. "It's an ongoing investigation. But don't worry DJ." "Easy for him to say." DJ thought. As he ushered DJ out of the room the officer leaned close and whispered "The napkin could be the key to everything."

CHAPTER 11

The ride back to Ren's studio had DJ's head spinning. What a morning. It was bad enough having to see the horrible scene of a dead body in the Cultural Gardens but to be considered a suspect and grilled by the Captain was unreal. He kept going over the events of the day as he drove which did nothing to improve his mood.

And what the heck did a generic napkin from the coffee shop have to do with anything. Was the killer's DNA on it? Were there fingerprints? What did it have to do with the murder?

DJ was mumbling to himself as he entered the studio and saw Ren perched on his chair staring at his screen. "So, Most Wanted Criminal," Ren chuckled "How did it go?" Peggy came over from the other side of the office to hear the story.

DJ told about the grilling from Captain Davenport and Ren could barely stifle a laugh as Peggy countered "Oh no. How terrible." Her tone was more sympathetic than before he left for the police station.

"I almost forgot the weirdest part," DJ jumped in. "As I was leaving, Officer O'Malley whispered something about the napkin being the key to everything."

"Yeah, that is weird. I'm glad I didn't use a napkin this morning," Ren added. "I don't remember if I did or not," offered Peggy "But I have probably used a lot of their napkins ever since I discovered their delicious green smoothie." "You mean a 'Peggy,'" Ren teased as

Peggy blushed. "I could use more than coffee to drink after this morning," DJ reflected.

The three friends sat in silence for a while, thinking. DJ tried to turn away from his fear of being a murder suspect to figuring out what was going on with a stupid napkin. As if on cue, he jumped up just as Ren was also leaping to his feet. "I've got it!" they shouted at once.

"Got what?" Peggy cried. "We have pictures and video of the crime scene," DJ offered. "We can go through the footage and see if there are any clues." "And maybe see if there is an incriminating napkin in any of the shots," Ren added.

The three planted themselves in front of three PCs and divided up the photos and videos to examine. They poured over the images making sure to zoom in on anything that was shot near the Hungarian Garden. It was tedious work and their eyes were getting strained but they pressed on.

DJ was working on the photos he took while Ren and Peggy were going through the videos – frame by frame. He eventually got to the photos near the Liszt monument that included the poor victim. The horrible memories of the scene made him want to stop but he pressed on, carefully viewing every section of the photos.

DJ was starting to go batty staring at essentially the same photo over and over and his eyes glazed over. He was about to hit the right arrow to go on to yet another image when he caught a tiny square of white. He sat up straight and zoomed in to that quadrant of the picture. He was glad he had shot all the images in the highest resolution available. Sure it took more SD cards but storage was cheap and swapping was easy.

He zoomed in and focused his eyes on part of a white square protruding from under the victim's neck. That was the "clue" that Officer O'Malley had rejected when DJ and Ren had pointed it out. One more zooming click and… it looked like a napkin!

DJ stared at the image. If he hadn't been asked by the police about a napkin he never would have spotted such a seemingly innocuous item. He still had no idea why it was important but he could tell that the napkin was about the same size and shape as what Captain Davenport had shown him. Only part of the napkin was visible but DJ was sure this was the same napkin.

"Hey guys," he shouted "I found something." Peggy and Ren

jumped up and crowded around DJ. "Zoom in, zoom in!" cried Ren. DJ centered his cursor on the white square and clicked zoom repeatedly. It definitely was a napkin and they could see the logo from the Cultural Gardens Coffee Shop. After one more zoom the trio could see some markings on the napkin.

DJ was glad that he always took multiple shots of each scene. He started doing that with people to make sure nobody was blinking but it soon became habit with all his shots. Hey, digital "film" was free so why not.

He clicked on the next shot of the same image and zoomed on the square of white. "It looks like there is something written on the napkin," DJ noted. One more zoom click and centering and they could make out some words.

The three looked at the screen and then looked at each other. The message they silently read explained why the police had asked DJ about the napkin. It was a message that certainly did not fit in the Cleveland Cultural Gardens. The words printed on the napkin that had been placed under the victim were clear: "You don't belong here."

CHAPTER 12

The three looked at each other and Peggy offered "That horrible message makes this sound like it's a hate crime! Everyone belongs in the Cultural Gardens. Diversity is what they are all about."

"We better let O'Malley know what we found," DJ said. Just then the studio phone rang and they all jumped. DJ answered and Officer O'Malley asked if they might have any images from the murder scene that they could look at. DJ hemmed and hawed but O'Malley said "I will be over in 5 minutes," and he hung up.

The three discussed what to do and just as they heard a car pull up they came to an agreement. "OK," DJ said, "We will help the investigation any way we can, but we won't just give them our content, right?" "Agreed," the other two echoed.

Officer O'Malley knocked on the studio door and Peggy let him in. "OK guys," he began "right now we don't have many clues to the murder. So we could use your help. Do you have any pictures of the scene we can look at?" DJ led him to the big display and showed the zoomed in image of the napkin. "We were just about to call you," he explained. "Sure, sure" said the cop.

O'Malley frowned. "So you know about the napkin and the message. You have to keep it quiet. This is an active investigation and if this leaks out it could prevent us from finding the killer." He paused. "Do you have an idea what that sentence means? You don't belong here? Is that why she was killed?"

"Who knows?" DJ replied. "It sounds like someone didn't want

26

this person in the Gardens." "Or was it that particular garden?" Ren asked. "Maybe they just didn't want her in the Hungarian Garden." Officer O'Malley frowned. "That's what we are afraid of," he said as Peggy nodded. "The note makes it sound like a potential hate crime rather than a random murder. We could have a big problem on our hands." He shook his head solemnly as he left the studio.

The next morning, DJ was jolted awake by his cell phone. He looked at the time – 5:30AM. And the caller – Officer O'Malley. Uh-oh. Now completely awake he ventured, "Yes Pat?" "I warned you" screamed the cop. "Why would you tell the press about the note? Captain Davenport wants to arrest you for interfering with an ongoing investigation!"

"What?" DJ replied, "I didn't say anything." "Then one of your cohorts did," countered O'Malley. "The Captain wants all 3 of you down at the station at 8AM." And the phone went dead.

DJ texted Ren and Peggy with the news. Ren's text back read "I just looked at the Cleveland Press website. You need to see it." DJ accessed the newspaper online and gulped at the headline: "You don't belong here – Murder in the Cultural Gardens." The article had a byline of Katrina DeSanto.

Reading through the article quickly DJ realized that Katrina didn't know much about the crime but she did have the info about the napkin and the note. But how? As far as he knew just Ren, Peggy and he knew about that except for the police. He was not looking forward to their meeting at the police station.

They decided to meet up before heading to their 8AM with the Captain. Peggy suggested the Cultural Gardens Coffee Shop but Ren and DJ both said "No way." Instead they met at Presti's bakery in Little Italy just above the Cultural Gardens.

Normally DJ would devour about 3 of the hot, fresh donuts but he didn't feel like it today. Peggy only nibbled at her scone but Ren not only wolfed down a few bear claws but he got a slice of the first pizza of the day to go. "Have to keep up my strength," he offered when they looked at him in surprise. "We didn't do anything wrong so we shouldn't be worried."

There wasn't much strategy to discuss as they had no idea how Katrina DeSanto had got that information. They only knew that it hadn't come from them. "You going to finish that?" Ren asked

Peggy as he eyed her uneaten scone. She gave him a look and shook her head no and the three headed out to their appointment.

Captain Davenport looked even angrier than usual as he entered the interrogation room. "I should arrest you all right now," he growled. "We didn't tell anyone Captain," DJ replied "We swear." "Then how did DeSanto get that information?" The three shrugged their shoulders.

"Look you three. You are in a lot of trouble. Leaking those details could prevent us from solving a terrible murder. Maybe a hate crime. What were you thinking?" The three all spoke at once again denying any responsibility.

The Captain raised his hand "Enough! I suggest you pull out your phones and look up the penalty for obstruction of justice," and he stormed out of the room.

Ten agonizing minutes later, Officer O'Malley came in. "I've been talking with the Captain," he said "and he isn't convinced yet but I am. I know you have had run-ins with DeSanto before and you don't exactly exchange Christmas cards. You wouldn't have tipped her off. I'll back you but you have to help me."

The three were witnessing a side of Officer O'Malley that they hadn't seen before – all business and a little scary.

"Help you how?" Peggy asked.

"I want you to go through all the footage you shot with a fine-tooth comb and report anything, and I mean anything, that is unusual or might be of interest, to me. Nobody else. Capisce? Now get out of here and get to work."

The three didn't have to be told twice. They jumped out of the chairs and headed to the parking lot. "Capisce?" Ren laughed. "O'Malley doesn't seem Italian to me."

Back at the studio they divided up the content and got to work. After a few hours DJ thought he was going cross-eyed from the staring. Suddenly Ren yelled "I got something," followed by "Uh oh."

DJ and Peggy gathered around the monitor. "This is from one of my drone cameras that I had set up unattended in record mode. I was hoping for some potential b-roll for the project." He pressed the play icon and chose slow motion. The screen showed the Liszt monument with a bulk behind it. They knew now, of course, that the bulk was the poor victim. "We've seen this already Ren," sighed

Peggy.

"Not this." Ren replied. "Watch this next part." In a few seconds a figure entered the screen and approached the tribute to Liszt. The figure knelt next to the body and pulled out what they now instantly recognized as a napkin from the Cultural Gardens Coffee Shop. A marker was produced and something was written on the napkin. Then the victim's hand was carefully lifted and the napkin was placed in it.

Then the figure crept away. The three were horrified. The images that Ren had captured could not be more clear. Yet they could not believe who was shown on the screen.

"It can't be!" DJ exclaimed. But it was. It was Angel Annie.

CHAPTER 13

Ren paused the screen and the trio stared in silence. "There must be a mistake." Peggy cried. "Annie wouldn't hurt anyone!" They all nodded in agreement. They replayed the video several times but there was no doubt that the figure placing the napkin with the message under the head of the victim was Angel Annie.

"This is just terrible," DJ said. "But we are going to have to tell O'Malley." "But Annie will be arrested," Peggy cried. "Maybe the video is wrong." "Tape don't lie," said Ren. "This is raw, unedited footage. It's 100% accurate."

After some more discussion, DJ called Officer O'Malley and suggested he get over to the studio on the double. They soon heard the squeals of the police car pull into the parking lot and O'Malley came rushing in. "What have you got?" he said breathlessly. "See for yourself," DJ replied.

Officer O'Malley watched the video. "Play it again," he barked. "Again" and he watched a third time. He had a pained expression on his face. With the Cultural Gardens as his beat he knew Annie better than anyone. In fact he was the one who christened her "Angel Annie." He had witnessed her cleaning up the litter of others and greeting everyone she met with her gentle voice. When he saw her give her own shabby coat to a shivering youngster a few winters ago he dubbed her "Angel Annie" and anyone who got to know her realized that it was the perfect name for her.

"I can't believe it," he whispered. "There must be some mistake." He finally snapped out of the reflective fog and grabbed for his radio.

"Captain?" he said "I need an arrest warrant. I'm going to pick up a suspect. It's Ang...It's Annie the homeless woman who frequents the Gardens."

Ren burned a copy of that part of the video to a flash drive and O'Malley shuffled out of the studio looking like he was on his way to a dental appointment. He turned and warned "Do NOT tell anyone about this – especially that Katrina DeSanto." And he was out the door.

The murder in the Cultural Gardens was the talk of the town. Nobody expected such a violent act in such a peaceful and historic place. A dedication ceremony for a new bust in the Serbian Cultural Garden the next day was overrun with media.

The Serbian Garden was only established recently – in 2008 – but it already had an impressive collection of busts including one of King Peter I who was known as the People's King and Liberator of Serbia. Nearby is a bust of Michael Pupin the Serbian scientist who received 34 patents for his inventions and won the Pulitzer Prize in 1924 for his autobiography.

The bust of Petar Petrovic Njegos honors the Bishop and Ruler who lifted the spirit of the Serbian people through his poetry.

One of the most popular busts was of Nikola Tesla, best known for many revolutionary contributions in the field of electricity and magnetism that formed the basis of modern alternating current electric power (AC) systems. In 1943, the Supreme Court of the United States credited him as being the inventor of the radio.

Across from Tesla is the bust honoring Mileva Maric the Serbian physicist and mathematician who was the wife and scientific partner of Albert Einstein. Another Serbian woman is also honored with a bust. Nadezda Petrovic was a Serbian painter from the late 19th and early 20th centuries.

The central part of the Serbian Garden is a tribute to Serbia's patron saint St. Sava. It was there that the media took root much to the dismay of Serbian Garden leaders Alex and his son Lex. Instead of asking about the famous figures of Serbian culture, the media, led by Katrina DeSanto, only seemed interested in talking about the murder.

The father-son duo deflected the questions as best they could. After all, it had happened in the Hungarian Garden about half a mile away. But as part of the Cleveland Cultural Gardens and the only garden with an event that day they were the target for the TV crews and reporters.

In a matter of minutes various beeps and ringtones sounded and the reporters all grabbed their cell phones as if synchronized and started packing up their gear and heading to their vehicles.

Alex and Lex and the crowd that had attended the event to honor Serbian culture were relieved and continued their ceremony. As the Kosovo Men's Choir began singing, they were wondering where the media had rushed off to.

The message that had been texted, tweeted and e-mailed was that the Cleveland Police had made an arrest in the case of the murder in the Cultural Gardens. Captain Davenport was going to be giving a press conference in 15 minutes in the Syrian Garden up the street on MLK. The Syrian Garden provided a built-in stage for the Captain to speak from.

The Syrian community joined the Cleveland Cultural Garden family with an official launch celebration on May 29, 2011. The central area contained a beautiful Arabic fountain which was surrounded by pedestals showcasing various aspects of Syria's history and culture.

There was also a bust of Syrian poet Nizar Qabbani but the highlight, and the reason for choosing this site for the press conference, was the replica of the Arch of Palmyra that served as a backdrop to a raised stage. The Monumental Arch also called the Arch of Triumph was an ornamental arch built by the Romans in the 3rd century. Its ruins became one of the main attractions of Palmyra but it was destroyed by the Islamic State of Iraq and the Levant (ISIL) in 2015. But the arch survived in the Syrian Cultural Garden.

Captain Davenport climbed the few levels and walked to the center of the Arch where a podium and microphones had been set up. The Captain looked solemn but somewhat proud as he stood at the microphone. He cleared his throat and began.

"Ladies and gentlemen. As you know a tragic act of violence took place on Saturday in one of the city's treasures, the Cultural Gardens. I am pleased to inform you that the hard work and expertise of the men and women of Cleveland PD has solved the crime and made an arrest. We have arrested a homeless woman who frequents the Gardens. Her name is Annie Adams and she is now in jail awaiting arraignment and trial."

"Is that Angel Annie?" Katrina DeSanto shouted. "I believe some have called her that," the Captain responded. "Why do you believe it was her? Was there a witness?" the reporter continued. "I can't comment on the case at this point but we have very solid evidence as to her guilt that will be made clear at her trial." "Has she confessed?" DeSanto pressed.

Davenport shuffled his feet and mumbled that she had denied committing the violent act. "Her public defender has advised her not to speak anymore. But, as I said, we have conclusive evidence against her and our department is confident in a swift conviction. The autopsy and evidence report will be available in about a week and you will see for yourself."

DeSanto and other reporters continued tossing out questions but the Captain's assistant sensed her boss' discomfort and ended the press conference. As he turned to leave the Captain heard a familiar, but not friendly, voice and stopped abruptly and wheeled around.

CHAPTER 14

Reginald Wilson, real estate developer (some would say land baron) in the nearby University Circle neighborhood stepped up to the microphone. He wore an expensive suit and the sun glinted off an expensive watch on his wrist. "Ladies and gentlemen of the media," he began. "Let me point out something that Captain Davenport neglected to mention. The so-called Cultural Gardens are a dangerous place for our citizens. All the statues and monuments, not to mention the trees and shrubs, make it an easy place for criminals to hide. And the Cleveland Police have only designated one officer, just one, to cover the entire 254 acres of the Gardens. And now some poor soul has paid the ultimate price."

His bald head shined in the sun and he mopped his brow with a silk handkerchief. "As I have stated before," he continued "the acreage should be sold to private developers who can modernize the space and make it safe and welcoming for all. While they talk about peace and diversity a poor African American woman was murdered because she "didn't belong there." I have a plan that will pay the City a substantial amount for the land and my company will provide rigorous security so tragedies like this murder won't happen again."

Wilson's right hand man, Theodore Mudhedge, began applauding like the Browns had just won the Super Bowl. He resembled a weasel both in appearance and actions.

"The Captain said this was just an isolated incident perpetrated by a homeless woman," interrupted Katrina DeSanto. "First of all,"

Wilson answered "Do you think this murderer is the only homeless person that frequents the Gardens? How many more of them are violent and dangerous and just waiting to attack innocent men, women and children? Are you willing to let your loved ones go to such a dangerous place? I'm not. My plan would make the area safe, not to mention prosperous."

"Hear hear!" cheered Mudhedge.

"That's enough!" barked Captain Davenport. "This is my press conference and I'll thank you to step away from MY microphone." "Certainly Captain," responded Reginald Wilson as he left the podium with a smile and began handing out papers with his development plan for the land to the assembled media. He knew it was too delicious for the reporters to ignore. His plan was coming together.

DJ was furious. He couldn't believe what he was reading in Katrina DeSanto's column the next day. She seemed to be making a case for Reginald Wilson's plan. Peggy practically sobbed "They wouldn't sell those beautiful Cultural Gardens to that Neanderthal Wilson would they? He would pave them over for a shopping mall and parking lots." They were on their way to meet with their client, Dr. Raselok, at Cleveland College.

Dr. Raselok looked morose as the trio entered his office. "This is terrible," he moaned. "First the murder and now that cretin Wilson and his plans to turn the Gardens into just another one of his condominium projects. Didn't he make enough money on the foreclosure crisis?"

Raselok really seemed to share their passion for the Cultural Gardens "Where else do you have a large statue of Mahatma Gandhi on a street named for Dr. Martin Luther King?" he would ask anyone who would listen. "Not to mention Mother Teresa in the Albanian Garden down the street and Copernicus, John Paul II and Madame Curie up the hill in the Polish Garden. These gardens are unique in the world and it's high time the world knew about them."

"Don't worry Doc," Ren replied "No way Reginald Wilson gets to buy the Gardens. And the murder is just an isolated incident that could happen anywhere in the city." "Actually," DJ added "the publicity of the murder is at least reminding people about the Gardens and getting people interested in them. Officer O'Malley said there were three times as many people in the Gardens today as usual. That weasel Mudhedge is really stirring the pot."

Peggy added "And, unfortunately, the story of Angel Annie and the murder got picked up by national media."

Raselok looked interested at their comments and then declared "OK, the project is still a go. Let's hope nothing else happens and let's tell the real story of this cultural treasure." The three let out a collective sigh of relief as they left the office.

"That was close," said DJ. "I thought he might pull the plug on the project. Just in case he changes his mind, let's get as much done as we can in the next few weeks." They each let their social media followers know of their plans for the next day in order to build buzz about the project and the Gardens. "Excited to cover the Lithuanian Garden tomorrow morning #culturalgardens" DJ tweeted.

The three concentrated on a few of the gardens on East Blvd. that morning. They stopped at the Gardens Coffee Shop at 99th and Superior for the usual drinks, except DJ went with a decaf. "What's the point?" Ren teased, sipping his high-test brew. Then they headed toward the Lithuanian Garden.

"It seems empty without Angel Annie here," said DJ. "I know," said Ren. "I can't believe she has been sitting in jail accused of murder. But the video shows her placing that note on the body." "Katrina DeSanto and the Cleveland Press have practically convicted her in print already. There's no way she can get a fair trial here," said DJ.

None of the three believed that the gentle Angel Annie could hurt anyone, let alone kill someone, but they had seen her on the video.

Their solemn reflection was broken by a commotion near the Italian Garden. The Italian Garden was one of the oldest and largest gardens. It was dedicated in 1930 and was designed in the spirit of the Italian Renaissance with large walkways, balustrades, benches and two large winding staircases leading down to a lower level amphitheater.

The upper level of the Italian Garden features a large Renaissance fountain modeled after the fountain in the Villa Medici in Rome. In 2008, the popular annual concert "Opera in the Italian Garden" was revived for the public, bringing back the original concerts in the garden during the 1940's. Italian Garden representative Joyce brought in local opera companies to perform famous music from well-known operas and it attracted thousands of attendees each year.

The upper level also includes a bust of the ancient Roman poet Virgil who wrote the "Aeneid." In 2012 a large bronze of Dante Alighieri, author of the Divine Comedy was dedicated. The Monte Grappa Boulder was a gift of the Italian government. The boulder was hewn from the side of Monte Grappa in northern Italy and honors Ohio veterans of the 332nd Regiment who fought on Italian soil in World War I.

Two large winding staircases lead to the lower level amphitheater and images of great Italian cultural figures in the Arts & Science and Arts & Letters such as: Michelangelo, Leonardo da Vinci, Giuseppe Verdi, Giotto, Petrarch and Guglielmo Marconi.

This morning the Italian Garden also featured an argument between Carl and Ernie. "Gentlemen, gentlemen," DJ shouted above the din. "What's the problem?" The two began speaking at once. "One at a time guys," said Ren. It turned out that the pair had been arguing about the murder.

It was a common occurrence. If Ernie said something was A, Carl would argue that it was B, and vice versa. The two didn't seem to realize that they were much more similar than different. They were both veterans, fiercely loyal to their heritage and the strongest supporters that the Cultural Gardens had. If they would just listen to each other for once they would have realized that they both agreed that Angel Annie was not a murderer and that soulless developers like Reginald Wilson should be driven out of town.

The five commiserated on the fact that they had been denied visitation privileges to see Angel Annie. They were told it could interfere with the case which didn't make sense to any of them.

After they calmed down, the pair went off to work in their own gardens and DJ, Ren and Peggy continued on to the Lithuanian Garden. Like the Italian Garden, the Lithuanian Garden had an upper level on East Blvd and a lower level on the east side of MLK Blvd.

The lower level featured a statue of Jonas Basanavicius, the founder of the first Lithuanian language newspaper Auszra. The Basanavicius statue was situated in front of The Pillars of Gediminas, one of the earliest symbols of Lithuania and one of its historical coats of arms.

The trio concentrated on the upper level which had busts of Maironis and Kudirka. Maciulis Maironis was one of the most famous Lithuanian romantic poets.

Vincas Kudirka was a Lithuanian poet and physician. He was also the author of both the music and lyrics of the Lithuanian National Anthem, Tautiška giesme, and is regarded in Lithuania as a National Hero.

They systematically did their work and after a while Ren said "I think we got it." The trio stated moving north to begin working on the next garden. All of a sudden, Peggy stopped. "What's that?" she cried in horror.

CHAPTER 15

Peggy pointed to the fountain that was the centerpiece of the upper level of the Lithuanian Cultural Garden. When they approached from the rear of the garden they could see a form lying behind the fountain. They scrambled over and gasped. It was a body!

"Oh no!" Peggy cried. They got closer and saw that the body was a light skinned middle aged woman. There was a pool of blood around her head. It was obvious that the woman was dead. "Oh my God!" cried Peggy. "Not another!"

The three stood frozen for a minute as they took in the horrible scene. They knew they couldn't help the victim and had learned not to touch anything so they slowly backed away unable to avert their eyes. Peggy was looking a little green and she rushed over to some bushes and bent over. DJ and Ren felt pretty much the same but managed to choke back the nausea.

DJ pulled out his cell and said "We better let O'Malley know. Ren, make sure you get pictures and video before he gets here and shoos us away." Ren had already been assembling his gear and began shooting images and video of the entire scene. "Uh-oh guys," Ren said. "Look at this."

Peggy managed to straighten up and joined DJ near the body behind the fountain. As their eyes focused on what Ren was pointing at they froze. It was a napkin from the Cultural Gardens Coffee Shop. It was placed under the head of the victim just like the first. As they got closer they saw the same familiar printing on the note: "You don't belong here."

Officer O'Malley did not look happy as he jumped out of his patrol car. "Don't tell me," he blurted. The trio pointed to the tragic scene and O'Malley looked visibly shaken. "Did you touch anything?" he asked. Assured that they had not he got on his radio and called the Captain. "Step back," he ordered as he began unwinding crime scene tape around the entire fountain and beyond. "The Captain is not going to be happy to see you."

And he wasn't. It was hard to determine if Captain Davenport was more upset at another dead body or that DJ, Ren and Peggy were involved. "You three always seem to be around bad news," he barked. "I want you all in my office in one hour - sharp."

Soon other police and emergency vehicles arrived and the trio made their way up East Blvd back to their car. They waited about half an hour before the Captain and Officer O'Malley came striding in and began grilling them about the morning's events.

"So it just happens to be you three again in the middle of a brutal murder. How do you explain that?" "You know we are working on a project in the Cultural Gardens, Captain," DJ replied. "We are there all the time." "Yeah but a lot of people visit the Gardens. Why is it that you three happen to discover murder victims?" the Captain questioned.

"Are you accusing us Captain? Your track record isn't so good in that respect." Ren pointed out. "What does that mean?" the Captain barked. "It means you are missing the big news!" Ren all but shouted.

What big news – besides another murder in the Cultural Gardens?" Officer O'Malley asked. Then DJ understood where Ren was going with this. "Think about it guys," DJ offered. "There was another murder in the Cultural Gardens. It looks like the same kind of attack. First of all, the second victim is white so these are probably not racially motivated attacks. And there was a note that appears to be identical to the one that was at the first crime scene."

"Tell us something we don't know," growled Davenport. "OK, how about this?" DJ countered. "It means you arrested the wrong person! Angel Annie has been locked up all week so there is no way she could have committed this murder. And it probably means she didn't commit the first one either. You have to let her go. The real killer is still out there."

Captain Davenport and Officer O'Malley looked at each other. "Not so fast," said the Captain. We have proof – thanks to you - of the homeless woman placing the note on the body. She had the means and opportunity and the note suggest her motive – that she didn't want others in her precious gardens."

"The video only shows her placing the napkin, not the murder," DJ replied. "There is no evidence that she did anything else. You have to let her go and go find the real killer."

The Captain stood up. "Finish giving your statements to Officer O'Malley and then get out of here. I don't want to see your faces anymore."

O'Malley looked a little relieved. "I think this bodes well for Annie," he said. "We should have the autopsy and forensic reports this afternoon and may be able to release Annie soon. But what was she doing there with the body and what's with the note she placed?"

"Can we talk with her?" Peggy asked. "The Captain won't like it but I may be able to swing it." O'Malley answered. "But don't tell anyone about what she says – especially Katrina DeSanto. And hey, be extra careful. It looks like we may have a serial killer out there."

CHAPTER 16

O'Malley led them to an area of the building that housed the prisoners before they were transferred to County or to a larger prison. They were seated in a drab room and a few minutes later he brought Angel Annie to them. They went to hug her but he jumped in. "No contact with the prisoner," he commanded using his official voice. "This has to be done by the book or we are all in big trouble."

Annie looked almost unrecognizable. They were used to seeing her in her big coat and floppy hat and gloves with the fingers cut off. Here she was in the jail's orange jumpsuit and it looks like she had showered and had a haircut. She looked like a completely different person, like someone you would see in an office or restaurant, not living on the streets. Each of the three was wondering to themselves what had happened to this poor woman to have her end up on the streets.

O'Malley told them they had ten minutes and to be careful as he exited the room. "Annie!" they all cried and began talking at once. "One at a time kids," she gushed. "First, how are you?" Peggy inquired. "Well I've slept in worse places and having 3 hot meals a day isn't so bad," she said "but I really miss being outside. I can't stand being confined. I miss my gardens!"

DJ jumped in. "We are so sorry Annie," he said "but we only have a few minutes to talk so I am going to get right to it. We know you didn't hurt that woman but the police have video showing you place that napkin with a note in your handwriting. What happened?"

Annie had a hard time keeping her concentration so DJ wanted her to tell her story before her mind wandered. She said "I was taking my morning constitutional and was picking up the trash that people had left behind. Why do people do that? Such a beautiful place and they leave their garbage behind, I don't get it. In fact one time..."

As she started to get off track DJ interrupted, "Please Annie tell us about the body." Annie seemed to focus and said "After talking with you that morning I went back to picking up trash and I noticed something behind the Liszt statue. I really love Liszt don't you? I can see why they had Lisztomania back in the day. He was quite a heartthrob. Did I tell you how I met Elvis once? He was..."

"Annie!" all three cried. "Tell us about the body!"

With a shake of her head Annie began again. I saw some red-brown liquid on the ground and thought that some kid had left their drink behind. I went over to check it out and pick up the cup if it was left when I saw her." Annie's eyes glazed over and her lips trembled. "We know this is hard Annie but please tell us what happened," Peggy begged.

"I went over to clean up the liquid when I saw a woman on the ground. She was so pretty and seemed so peaceful. But when I got closer I saw that part of her head was hurt and it wasn't a spilled drink but blood on the ground. I felt so bad for her. She was so young and innocent. And in the Cultural Gardens of all places. I didn't know what to do. I couldn't help her and I am not exactly best friends with the police, though O'Malley isn't too bad, but I couldn't just leave her there. I knelt by the poor creature and said a prayer. I looked through my treasures that I had picked up that morning and found a napkin from the coffee shop. I took out my pen, the one my son gave me all those years ago, and wrote on it. Did I ever tell you about my son? He is..."

"Annie! Why did you write 'You don't belong here'?" DJ asked.

"Well, she didn't," Annie replied. "She was so young and innocent and the Gardens are a place of peace. She didn't belong there and I wanted her and everyone else to know it."

The three said goodbye to Angel Annie when O'Malley came back and assured her that she would be back in her beloved gardens soon. They relayed the story she had told them and O'Malley nodded with understanding. "That makes sense," he opined. "If the forensics collaborate her story she should be released soon."

The four walked excitedly back to the parking lot and Pat O'Malley asked "Do me a favor. Go through all your footage one more time. We have a serial killer out there and he's smart enough to make this murder look like the other by copying Angel Annie's note on the napkin. Maybe he messed up and there is some clue in your photos or videos."

Ren complained "My eyeballs are already fried but we'll do it Pat."

"Do what?" a voice asked? It was Katrina DeSanto. She was scribbling in her reporter's notebook with her left hand and had her cellphone in record mode in the right hand. "None of your concern Ms. DeSanto" O'Malley replied. "The press has a right to know. My scanner picked up the call this morning. Is there a serial killer in the Cultural Gardens?"

"You'll have to talk to the Captain," O'Malley answered and turned and walked rapidly back to the station house. "Well?" the reporter asked of the three who remained. "I hear that this murder was just like the first – down to the details. What do you know?"

"We don't know anything," DJ replied and they headed to the car. "You can't run from the press!" DeSanto shouted after them. "You will be sorry."

CHAPTER 17

And sorry they were when they read the reporter's Twitter posts later that day. "Why are Jamieson, Wu and Powell always in the middle of trouble? #involved?" read one tweet. The trio had a long history with the reporter both individually and even more so when they had formed their startup. They had naively believed that "off the record" meant just that and their attempt to assist in a story last year had come back to bite them.

The tweets from Reginald Wilson were even worse. "The Cultural Gardens are a dangerous place with a serial killer roaming free. Time to shut them down before another murder. #shutthemdown."

And "If the police can't protect us in this so-called park it's time to let our private security force make us safe again. #shutthemdown."

Of course Wilson's lackey Theodore Mudhedge retweeted and favorited every post and while he had few followers, he bought a lot of "likes."

"This stinks," said Ren. "Two admittedly terrible acts by one psycho and they act like the Gardens are a terror zone. We're there every day and it's the same old peaceful Gardens. Maybe if we do some positive social media posts during and after our shoot today that will help."

"I hope Dr. Raselok doesn't get discouraged and pull the plug on our project," Peggy added.

The three gathered their gear and headed back to the Gardens. The upper level still had some crime scene tape and some looky-loos wanting to see the site of a murder so they headed south on MLK.

The southernmost garden was the Chinese Garden. It was separated from the other gardens by about ½ mile. The Chinese community chose that location because it was closer to the Cleveland Museum of Art and some of the other cultural institutions of University Circle. Their vision was beginning to prove sound as new gardens were being planned for the space between the Chinese Garden and the rest. The Ethiopian community already had a plot selected nearby and had dedicated a beautiful large wall displaying 5,000 years of history. The Colombians, Uzbeks and French were interested in a plot of land nearby too.

The Chinese Cultural Garden was dedicated on April 1, 1985. It was a gift of the city of Tapei and its business community and was modeled after the Chinese Imperial Palace. The plaque acknowledging the gift says: "On behalf of the people of Taipei We present this Chinese Cultural Garden to the people of Cleveland as a confirmation of friends and cultural exchange between our sister cities." It is a beautiful plot of land featuring two large dragon statues "protecting" the space.

A large bright white raised area is covered in detailed ornamentation and is the site of the highlight of the Garden, a larger than life granite statue of the great philosopher and teacher Confucius who watches over the garden. Each year the Chinese community of Cleveland plants a cherry tree in honor of teachers on Confucius' birthday.

The three posted selfies with Confucius to their Instagram accounts and lots of other pictures and positive comments about the beautiful garden. They spent several hours chronicling every inch of the Garden. Though none of them said anything they all were privately relieved that there were no victims or any problems discovered. Maybe the killings would stop at the two that were already committed.

They went back to the studio and started posting positive tweets and photos to their social media accounts encouraging people to continue to visit and support the Gardens. Combined, their social media reach was at least as large as that of DeSanto and what Wilson could buy.

They felt good about the last few hours especially when their client, Dr. Raselok called to congratulate them. "Good work guys," the professor said. "I'm seeing a lot of retweets and likes on your posts. We can't let people be scared to go to the Gardens."

"Thanks Doc," DJ answered. "As you saw in our posts, we will be working the south of MLK tomorrow morning starting with the Irish and Indian gardens." DJ, Ren and Peggy separated and headed to their homes with a feeling of accomplishment. They had a busy morning planned so were looking forward to a restful night.

Unfortunately, that was not going to be the case.

CHAPTER 18

All 3 phones buzzed at the same time at 6:30 AM the next day. The group text was from Officer Pat O'Malley and it was short, if not sweet. "Get down to the Chinese Garden now!"

They each got dressed, grabbed their gear and headed to the Chinese Garden with a bad feeling in their stomachs. Their worst fears were realized as they saw several police and emergency vehicles. "Pat, what happened?" DJ asked as they rushed up to the crime scene tape. They spotted the Captain by the Confucius statue glaring at them. His features seemed as hard as the granite in the statue.

"Another murder," O'Malley answered. "A tai chi group meets here early every morning and they spotted the body of a white male behind the statue." "Oh no," Peggy moaned. "Even worse," the officer continued, "the Captain heard about your social media posts about the Chinese Garden and is not happy with you three."

"Was there a note?" Ren asked. "Is it the same guy?" O'Malley was about to answer when he stopped abruptly. Katrina DeSanto was rushing over, audio recorder in hand. "What's the story, O'Malley?" the reporter queried. The officer told her to talk to the Captain and slunk away.

The reporter turned toward the three. "So you guys flood Instagram encouraging people to visit the Chinese Garden and someone gets killed here. How does that make you feel?" she asked thrusting the recorder in DJ's face. "Get lost Katrina," Ren replied and the three went to the other side of the garden.

"This is not good," said Ren. O'Malley quietly returned to the group and suggested "If I were you I'd get the heck out of here. We will call you later to come in for questioning."

"But Pat," DJ asked. "Is it the same killer?"

O'Malley looked around to make sure nobody else was listening and whispered "Same MO, same note, same killer."

It was tough doing their work that morning but the trio ventured down to the Irish Garden anyway. They felt somehow responsible for the murder since they had posted so much about the Chinese Garden the day before.

The Irish Cultural Garden was one of the oldest gardens. Initial fundraising by the Irish Cultural Garden League began in 1933 and the completed garden was formally dedicated in 1939. Many visitors did not realize that the garden's sandstone pathways are arranged in the shape of a Celtic cross. Like many of the older Cultural Gardens the Irish Garden suffered from some neglect for a period of years but had been revitalized over the past decade or so.

Peggy pointed out a magnificent oak tree that remains from the 1930's and continues to shade the garden. The original plantings included Irish blackthorn, used in the making of the shillelagh. DJ and Ren were again surprised and impressed by their colleague's knowledge. Peggy tried to cover up her grin.

In 2010 a grand new addition to the Irish Garden was dedicated - a 3-piece, 13,000-pound granite fountain that is a duplicate of a fountain in Dublin, Ireland. As you venture through the Garden there are monuments to Irish cultural heroes such as William Butler Yeats, Padraic Pearse, Oliver Wendell Holmes, James Joyce, Edna O'Brien, John Millington Synge, George Bernard Shaw, Sean O'Casey, Samuel Beckett, and others.

The Irish community is large and strong in Cleveland and the Irish Garden Club, as they called themselves, had taken the Garden under their wing. Eddie, Char, Jack, Sheila, Martin, Bill, Jim and others had since hosted numerous concerts and events including a visit from the Taoiseach (Prime Minister) of Ireland a few years ago. It was one of DJ's favorite gardens but what should have been an enjoyable few hours was tempered by the events earlier that morning.

"Could we be responsible for the killing?" Peggy finally asked out loud what they all had been thinking. They had all been considering what their role might have been. After all, just hours earlier they had announced how the Chinese Garden was such a cool destination. And now someone was dead.

"We don't know if the victim or the killer saw our posts or even know that we exist," DJ answered. "It could be a terrible coincidence. But we have to be careful and assume that the killer is monitoring our posts. Let's get whatever work done that we can because I'm sure Captain Davenport will be summoning us soon." And he was right.

They crossed Superior Ave and methodically documented the Syrian Garden before crossing a busy MLK Boulevard. That land was designated for the future homes of both the Pakistani and Lebanese Gardens. The Lebanese Garden already has a flower bed in the form of the Lebanese flag – red and white with the cedar tree in the middle. Pierre, Tony, Faris, Abby and others had big plans for the Garden.

Qaisra, Madiha and others in the Pakistani community hung a huge green and white flag of Pakistan in the garden when they hosted events.

Though neither the Pakistani or Lebanese gardens were officially dedicated yet, they were already very active gardens as hundreds from their communities showed off their food, culture and performances to thousands of people at the annual One World Day event.

One World Day was the biggest annual event in the Cultural Gardens. Since 1945 the Cleveland Cultural Gardens Federation has hosted an annual event called One World Day. The purpose of One World Day was to bring people to see all the Gardens and celebrate together.

One World Day featured ethnic performances and food in all the gardens and thousands, sometimes tens of thousands, of people came and took part. One of the two highlights of the day was the Naturalization ceremony where a Federal Judge came to one of the gardens and about 25 people from all over the world swore their oath of citizenship in a moving and inspiring ceremony.

The other highlight was the Parade of Flags. Each of the gardens, and many communities that did not yet have a garden, gathered for a parade that featured them marching in their ethnic costumes and carrying the flags of their ancestral homes.

The Parade of Flags resembled an Olympics opening ceremony

with a girl scout or other youngster leading each group with a sign saying "Italian" or "German" or "Latvian" and so on. The Parade was growing each year and was a clear demonstration of the diversity of heritages of the people of Cleveland. The hope was to eventually have all 120 or so ethnic communities represented by people of the city march in the Parade of Flags.

In the last few years crowds of 20,000 to 30,000 attended One World Day and even more were expected this year. And that terrified DJ.

Nobody had said it out loud yet but they had all been thinking about the upcoming One World Day. What if the killer was not caught by then? Would people feel safe coming to the event and bringing their families? Would ethnic communities want to come and march in the parade?

DJ wondered to himself if maybe the killings had something to do with the rapidly approaching One World Day. If the event was cancelled because of safety concerns it would be a shame after 75 such annual events. It would also give Reginald Wilson more ammunition to turn the Gardens into his shopping mall/apartments/parking lot. DJ was determined to not let that happen.

He cleared his mind and joined the other at the next garden. It was one of the most popular gardens, the India Garden. When you say "Indians" in Cleveland the first thought is probably the baseball team. The Cleveland Indians had been playing major league baseball since 1901.

But there was another Cleveland Indians. The Indian community was large and successful. Many were engineers, doctors and other highly regarded professions. They dedicated the India Garden in 2006 and unveiled and dedicated what has become one of the most popular statues in the Cultural Gardens.

The statue of Mahatma Gandhi on the granite pedestal stands 17' tall. The pose was familiar to those who saw the movie "Gandhi" – Gandhi with a walking stick on his way to the salt protest.

Ren read aloud a quote from the one side of the Mahatma Gandhi statue: "Ahimsa (Non-violence) is the greatest force at the disposal of mankind. It is mightier than the mightiest weapon of destruction devised by the ingenuity of man." The three reflected solemnly on these powerful words in this peaceful place in light of the recent violence.

When the statue of Gandhi was dedicated, the Ambassador of India came for the ceremony. Later the grandson of the Mahatma, Rajmohan Gandhi, visited and planted a tree in his grandfather's honor. Crowds marveled at the large statue of Gandhi located on a street named for Dr. Martin Luther King Jr. Dr. King had visited Gandhi in India and their shared visions of non-violence linked them forever. And now they were also linked on the streets of Cleveland.

The India Garden also contained six Heritage Pillars depicting India's contributions to humanity, Artistic Traditions, Leaders and more. Each pillar depicts a lotus flower in relief. Peggy pointed out that the lotus is the national flower of India.

With a population of well over 1 billion there were dozens of languages spoken and religions practiced. Inscriptions in the walkway at the entrance to the garden say "Welcome" in 15 of India's major languages as well as English.

The India Garden offers a calming experience under the gaze of the Mahatma and you could find people learning and doing yoga there on One World Day and other days.

In some ways, the India Garden was the catalyst for a resurgence in the entire chain of Cultural Gardens. Some of the gardens had been neglected and vandals and thieves had stolen busts to salvage bronze or other metals. But when Gandhi appeared on the street it seemed to invigorate other communities to improve their gardens or start a new one.

DJ was hoping that the presence of Gandhi might lead to an end of this rash of violence in the Gardens. But he wasn't optimistic.

CHAPTER 19

DJ recalled that Ernie and some others had never been happy that the street name was changed from Liberty to MLK Boulevard. It was nothing against Dr. King. They knew that the street had originally been named Liberty Boulevard to honor those who fought in World War I to bring liberty to the world.

DJ's mind raced. Could one of those people be behind the murders? The phrase "You don't belong here" could be the grumblings of a reactionary person who was witnessing new types of people join "his or her" beloved Gardens.

DJ shook his head as if to clear it. No way Ernie would be behind something like this. He had witnessed a lot in his long life and had often professed his admiration for peacemakers like Gandhi and Dr. King. He and Carl, two stubborn opinionated guys, had a lot more in common than they thought. Hhhm. Could Carl be telling some of the new communities from the Middle East and Asia that they don't belong here?

"OK DJ," he thought to himself. "You need some sleep. These wild thoughts are impossible. The victims were of various races and genders. Plus, Angel Annie had already explained the reasoning of that phrase – at least its original intent." As they gathered their gear and drove down the street DJ spotted Carl and Ernie having one of their spirited but friendly discussions near the Cultural Gardens

Visitors Kiosk.

"Solving the problems of the world again guys?" he shouted as he slowed to a stop in front of them. They both shouted back something about trying to convince this bullheaded person about something. They then slapped each other on the back and resumed their banter. DJ was reassured that Carl and Ernie were not involved in the murders but in the back of his mind he still wondered if one of their cohorts might be more extreme – and wiling to kill to protect "their" Gardens.

After finishing the work in the India Garden, the three needed some advice and decided to check in with their sponsor Dr. Raselok. The professor picked up on the third ring and was greeted by DJ, Ren and Peggy on speaker. They gave him an update on their progress and he seemed pleased. "If you keep up this pace you will be finished by One World Day," the professor explained. "Then once you document that day we can do the final editing and publish!" The excitement was evident in his voice. "We can even have pre-sale flyers in a booth at One World Day."

"Sounds like a plan," DJ replied "but we have a couple of concerns. We know we are supposed to be flooding our social media accounts with our progress to build up a buzz for the final project. But, as you know, when we posted about the Chinese Garden there was a murder there the next day. What if our posts caused that to happen? We don't want to do posts of today's work and have someone else get hurt or killed."

The professor's excitement tempered. "You have to continue posting," he said. "Even more than ever. Otherwise the bad guys win. In fact we should buy some promo ads on Twitter and Facebook to take advantage of the Gardens being in the news. The Cultural Gardens are trending on social media and we can leverage that." There was a pause and Peggy blurted out "But it seems ghoulish to try and take advantage of these tragedies."

Raselok's tone softened. "You are right to be concerned Peggy but you have to look at the bigger picture. The murders have already taken place – it's a terrible tragedy. But we have a chance to use that tragedy for good. We can share the wonderful story of the Cultural Gardens with thousands of new people who would never know about them. All with a few hashtags and posts. We can't bring those poor souls back to life but we can make sure that something good comes out of their demise,"

It was not easy to accept but that argument seemed to make sense to the trio. "Okay," said DJ "we will keep posting. But maybe we should let Officer O'Malley know which gardens we will be posting about so he can beef up patrols around them. We don't want to be responsible in any way for another murder."

"Good idea," replied the professor. "I can't wait to see your Instagram feeds later today. The India Garden is one of my favorites. Keep up the great work." And he hung up. But it wasn't their social media that was about to get all the attention.

It seemed like every other posting on social media was either from the Cleveland Press, specifically Katrina DeSanto, or a sponsored posting from Theodore Mudhedge or other people that had to be working for Reginald Wilson. Wilson and his cronies were spreading the idea that the Gardens were dangerous and warning people to stay away.

"If you care about your family's lives, stay away from the Cultural Gardens! #murderintheculturalgardens" was a representative tweet. Ren checked some statistics and groaned "That hashtag is trending. And not just in Northeast Ohio. It looks like AP has picked up the Cleveland Press feed and is distributing it all over."

Peggy found an article on a popular national blog that was blaming racism and fear of immigrants for the murders. They had focused on the "You don't belong here" message as their rationale. Though its origin had been explained by Angel Annie they proclaimed that the copycat killer must have agreed with the message and claimed it as his own.

She read a quote from Theodore Mudhedge and when she scrolled down she was startled by the byline – Katrina DeSanto. So DeSanto was using these tragic events to make a name for herself nationally. "That is so like her," she grumbled.

They knew that their own positive posts were going to get lost in the storm of posts from DeSanto and Wilson and Mudhedge but began sending anyway. "Let's face it; bad news is more interesting than positive stuff." Ren commented. But they knew it was a losing battle today. Few would click through to posts about the majestic India Garden when they could choose some negative click bait like the others were posting.

Ren was scrolling on his phone, Peggy on a tablet and DJ on a PC and they all saw the same post at the same time. There was a collective gasp.

The tweet came from Reginald Wilson and included the offensive hashtag. But it was the body of the message, in all caps no less, that shocked them. It read "ONE WORLD DAY HAS BEEN CANCELLED DUE TO THE CULTURAL GARDENS BEING DANGEROUS!"

CHAPTER 20

It couldn't be. Had the Cultural Gardens Federation really cancelled One World Day after almost 80 years of holding it every year?

They clicked on the link in the tweet and were redirected to a webpage which had obviously been put together quickly. It echoed the tweet in the headline. As they read they saw that it was a message from Reginald Wilson as follows:

"ONE WORLD DAY HAS BEEN CANCELLED DUE TO THE CULTURAL GARDENS BEING DANGEROUS! That's what the headline in the Cleveland Press should read. Cleveland Police and the Cleveland Cultural Gardens Federation have been unable to insure the safety of the public. But they want tens of thousands of citizen to risk their lives for their event.

What is more important? The safety of you and your family or some outdated party in a dangerous area of the city? It's a shame that this land that businessman and entrepreneur John D. Rockefeller left to the city has been wasted for all these years. It could be the source of jobs for our citizens and a safe place to live and shop. My plan will make that happen. That's what John D. Rockefeller would want.

Let the Mayor know that you value your family's safety. Attend our upcoming 'Rally for Safety in Rockefeller Park". We will provide security which is more than we can say about the police department unfortunately. Exact date, time and location to be announced soon.

Sign up below to be kept informed or just show up. Make your voice heard in our call for progress and prosperity instead of murder and fear."

Below the text there was a picture of a smiling Reginald Wilson with his lackey Theodore Mudhedge surrounded by workers in hard hats with their thumbs up. Next to that was a black and white image of the crime scene tape around the Liszt monument in the Hungarian Garden.

"I have to admit," Ren said "That's an effective campaign. He can afford to buy a lot of views and likes too." "I wonder how many will show up for his rally," Peggy asked. "I'm more concerned with how many won't show up for One World Day," DJ replied, and he did not look pleased.

The first thing the three did the next morning when they got out of bed was check the news, hoping that there weren't any more problems in the Gardens. Nothing seemed to have happened and that was confirmed when Officer O'Malley called DJ a little after 8:30. "A quiet night in the Gardens DJ," O'Malley offered. "But the Captain and I want you to come by the station later this morning for another, uh, chat."

DJ agreed and then quickly scanned the Cleveland Press online looking for any updates. Katrina DeSanto had an interview with Reginald Wilson which made him look like the only one who cared about the safety of the public. He framed his recommendation to sell and repurpose the Gardens as if he was a combination of Mother Teresa and John D. Rockefeller themselves.

DJ filled in the others on their way to the day's work in the Gardens. They were working their way down MLK and started at the Croatian Garden. The Croatian Garden had both an upper level on East Blvd and a lower level on MLK. They were connected by a cascading stream running down the hill. The lower level of the Croatian Garden was one of DJ's favorites because of the Immigrant Mother statue. The Immigrant Mother statue was sculpted by a talented, now deceased, sculptor named Joseph Turkaly who had made many sculptures that could be seen around town.

While most Gardens featured monuments to cultural figures of their own heritage, the Immigrant Mother represented all the women who left their homelands, often with children in tow, to come to America. They were often separated from their husbands who had gone earlier to find work and the duties and hardships of bringing the rest of their family from the only home they ever knew.

DJ always appreciated the fact that the Croatian community could have put up a monument to a Croatian cultural hero but instead chose to honor all the immigrant mothers who gave up so much to start a new life for their family in America. DJ was considering using an image of the Immigrant Mother for the cover of their project because it really captured the spirit of all the Gardens.

The Croatian Garden was one of the newer gardens. Ground was broken in 2011. The growth and development of the Cultural Gardens was a mirror of the growth of the population of Cleveland and all of the US. The early gardens were mostly European because those communities had come to Cleveland earlier and became established. As time marched on people from all over the world made their way to the US and Cleveland and soon there was interest in gardens from communities representing Asia, the Middle East, Africa and South America.

World events played a part in the growth of the Gardens as well. For example, there had originally been a Yugoslav Garden but when Yugoslavia split up it became the Slovenian Garden. Communities once under the umbrella of the Soviet Union like Lithuania, Latvia, Estonia and Ukraine had their own gardens.

The African American Garden was progressing and there were solid plans underway for the first gardens representing Hispanic heritages. The Colombian community had already submitted plans. As the 120 or so distinct ethnic groups represented in Cleveland established their communities they often looked to establish a Cultural Garden. DJ just hoped that someone from an earlier established community wasn't telling newcomers that they "don't belong here" with murder.

The crew quickly covered the lower half (on MLK Blvd) of the Hebrew, British and German Gardens. Outside of some beautiful landscaping the major cultural monuments of those gardens were on their upper levels on East Blvd.

After several more hours Ren's smart watch beeped. He rolled up to the other two on his hoverboard and reminded them, "Time to go to jail!" Their feelings of accomplishment after a productive morning of work soon turned to dread as they knew they would soon be sitting across from Captain Davenport.

The three checked in at the front desk and since they were becoming regulars at the station they knew right where to go. The interrogation room was set up to be intimidating and it still felt that way to the trio. "Talk about scared straight," Peggy commented. "We haven't even done anything and I am going to make sure I never sit in a room like this again."

DJ caught Ren's eye and the two burst out laughing. "You won't even jaywalk," Ren laughed. "And you pick up other people's litter," DJ added. "And you always drive 5 miles below the speed limit," Ren continued. They kept adding testaments to the unlikeliness of Peggy ever being arrested and the laughter grew. Even Peggy who had seemed annoyed at first now started to chuckle. When her chuckle turned into an embarrassing snort, all three lost it.

"I wouldn't think you'd be having such a good time with three dead bodies," Captain Davenport bellowed as he opened the door and burst into the room. The laughter immediately stopped and their faces turned solemn. Officer O'Malley looked solemn too and the two law enforcement officers sat down across from the three.

"Against my better judgment," the Captain began looking sideways at O'Malley, "I have decided to share some information about the murders in the Cultural Gardens with you three in the hope of getting some quicker results. As you know, this has become a political football with Reginald Wilson and the Cleveland Press taking every opportunity to make the Mayor and the Cleveland PD look bad. Officer O'Malley has told me that you three know the Cleveland Cultural Gardens and the regulars who frequent it as much as anyone. Is that so?"

"Yes sir," they all echoed. "Officer O'Malley has indicated that there are several people who frequent certain areas of the Gardens that we may want to speak to. Obviously we have spoken to the woman you refer to as Angel Annie and her alibi is sound. Who else is a regular in the Gardens?

The three hesitated. "Look Captain," DJ finally began. "We know all the regulars and we know that none of them could be responsible for these murders. We don't want to tell you about them and have you interrogate them or worse. Look at what happened to Angel Annie."

O'Malley chimed in. "Trust me. We are not looking to pin this on one of them. We just want to talk to them and see if they remember anything or noticed anything out of the ordinary. In fact, they may be more open in talking with you three than us. Will you help us?"

The three exchanged glances and Ren answered "OK but if we help you, you have to do something for us." The Captain's neck started to turn red and before he exploded Officer O'Malley jumped in and asked "What are you looking for?"

"As you have acknowledged," DJ began "we know the Cultural Gardens about as well as anyone. Many people know their own gardens better than us but for the Gardens as a whole we are your best bet. We probably walked every inch of the 254 acres even before we began this project with Dr. Raselok at Cleveland University. Now we not only have our memories but a lot of notes, photos and videos. We hate seeing these tragic murders scare people away from the Gardens. And we hate Wilson's plans to turn them into another one of his strip malls." He paused and accepted nods of confirmation from Ren and Peggy.

"So," he continued, "we are willing to share our information if you share your information with us. We want to act as a team and find this killer soon. One World Day is approaching."

"You dare to bargain with the Cleveland Police Department," the Captain huffed. "We can get a court order and confiscate your content."

"I don' think so Captain," DJ replied, "and the odds of there being anything useful in the hundreds of hours of video and tens of thousands of photos we have are slim and none." "And Slim just left the building," Ren quipped to the glare of the Captain.

"What you really need is our familiarity with the Gardens and the people who frequent them. And we are more than willing to help Pat with any information we can. But we think that we could be really useful if we had some of your information."

"Like what?" barked the Captain.

"Like the autopsy and forensic reports," Peggy answered.

CHAPTER 21

All eyes turned to Peggy who was usually the silent one at these meetings. She blushed at the attention and then continued "If both of us have all the available information we can, working as a team, solve these murders." The room was silent and then Captain Davenport replied.

"Okay. This is how it is going to work. Officer O'Malley will be your liaison with the department on this case. You will share any and all information you have with him and he will direct the relevant facts to me. In turn, he will provide you with details that CPD may possess that may be valuable to you. On one condition. Anything we share with you has to be kept private. No social media postings, no discussion with anyone else and certainly nothing shared with Katrina DeSanto or any other media. Agreed?"

The three looked at each other and nodded. "Agreed," they proclaimed.

Captain Davenport stood up. "I'll let you four get to work while I go get chewed out by the Chief and the Mayor again." When he left the room Officer O'Malley grinned and said "Saints preserve us. I never thought I'd see the day when hardcore Daniel 'Stonewall' Davenport would agree to something like this. Peggy I think you clinched the deal!" And they all laughed as Peggy's face grew crimson.

"Okay," O'Malley said "Let's get started. Who are the people you see regularly in the Gardens that might be able to help?" He took out a legal pad and began writing as the trio offered names. Angel Annie, of course. Ernie from the Hungarian Garden is retired and always working on both levels. Carl Jefferson is also retired and spends most days in the African-American Garden.

"Those two are very opinionated and possessive of "their"

gardens but rarely venture outside their own spaces," DJ added. "They know every square inch of their gardens but are oblivious to any others so they probably won't have much information to offer."

"Since we are sharing information," O'Malley replied, "We have had several complaints about both of these guys. Basically it's from people they have chased away who were doing something in 'their' gardens that they didn't approve of. The complaints fit the pattern of 'You don't belong here'."

"Carl and Ernie can be hard guys," Ren pointed out "but they would never murder someone." "They are both veterans," O'Malley continued "and both are registered gun owners so we have to keep them on the suspect list." "But the victims weren't shot," all 3 blurted out at the same time. "I know," the cop replied "but they stay on the suspect list until they are cleared. Now who else is always in the Gardens?"

"Most of the regulars are like Ernie and Carl. They work in their own Gardens. Paul is always in the Czech Garden. Lex is in the Serbian, Tom in the Croatian, Boris and Svetlana in the Russian, Char and Sheila in the Irish, Kevan in the Armenian, Mehmet in the Turkish, Gary and Connie in the Polish, Pierre in the Lebanese, Wael in the Syrian and so on."

O'Malley wrote feverishly but DJ cautioned him. "Most of the regulars are also members of the Cleveland Cultural Gardens Federation so they follow the Federation's motto of 'Peace through mutual understanding' and would never tell anyone 'You don't belong here' let alone kill anyone."

Officer O'Malley still wanted the full names of all the regulars but agreed to let the three talk to each instead of him interrogating them officially. Nobody thought there was the slightest chance that any of these dedicated volunteers could be a serial killer. They were passionate volunteers.

Very few people realized that all the monuments and statues in the Gardens, along with the maintenance and sprucing up, were because of volunteers. They raised money, spent long hours with city planning commissions and implemented the plans. Then they were responsible for maintenance and upkeep as well as hosting events in their gardens. Such ardent volunteers were not of the temperament to exclude anyone let alone harm them.

This continued for a while and soon Officer O'Malley's legal pad was full. "Ok Pat," DJ said. "We did our part – now what do you have for us?" The officer opened a briefcase and pulled out a couple of folders. "This is really going to surprise you," he predicted. And it did.

"Remember, this is all top secret," O'Malley warned as he opened the first folder. It was the autopsy report and forensics from the first murder. "As expected," he began "the cause of death was a blow to the head with a nondescript blunt object. The victim most likely died instantly. There was no sign of a struggle or defensive wounds. Now comes the interesting part."

The three leaned forward as one as if they were attached. "The Medical Examiner says the time of death was about 36 hours before Angel Annie and then you found her." "No way," interjected Ren. "We shot in the Hungarian Garden the day before and were all around the Liszt monument and there was no body there."

"Let me continue," O'Malley said. "The victim's fingerprints were not on file but preliminary correspondence with a dentist indicate that the victim's teeth matched the dental records of a woman from Youngstown. Youngstown PD had a missing person's report on someone resembling our victim and have an all-points bulletin out on her boyfriend."

"Sorry Pat," Peggy said "But this doesn't make any sense. How does a missing person from Youngstown connect with the serial killer in the Cleveland Cultural Gardens?"

"Let me continue," Pat said a little less patiently than before. "I told you this is where it gets interesting. We believe that our victim was a young woman who lived in Youngstown with her good-for-nothing boyfriend. The boyfriend has a long rap sheet – drugs and violent behavior. He conveniently has not been seen since our first victim was killed."

O'Malley continued despite the puzzled looks. "Both Cleveland and Youngstown PD believe this repeat offender killed his girlfriend for whatever reason and then dumped her in the Cultural Gardens."

"But…" all three started but O'Malley raised his hand to stop them. "Why does a Youngstown creep dump a body in the Cleveland Cultural Gardens?" He paused for effect. "Because he was born and raised on St Clair Ave. right here in the Gardens. So he knew the area intimately and must have figured that nobody would ever look for a Youngstown victim hidden in a Cleveland park. But our forensics staff proved him wrong."

There was silence for a minute and then DJ asked "Do you mean that a Youngstown criminal killed someone and dumped her body and then has killed 2 other people here?"

"Nope. This is where it really gets interesting," O'Malley answered. "We are now convinced that there is a copycat killer."

"Whoa," said Ren. "That's crazy. Maybe it's just the same evil dude who came back home to his old neighborhood and decided to keep killing."

Officer O'Malley leaned forward and reminded the three that the information he was sharing was not to be mentioned to anyone. "The Medical Examiner says that while the assaults are similar – blunt object to the head – there are inconsistencies with the first murder and the other two."

"Inconsistencies?" Peggy asked. "Like what?" "Well, for one," Pat replied "the angle of the blow was different in the first murder than in the others. The second and third murders have other details that connect them but are different from the first one."

"Such as?" Ren prodded. "Such as probable height of the attacker and it's likely that the dominant hand of the first killer was his right while the copycat appears to be a leftie."

This was a lot to digest so all four sat in silence for a while. "So what's the plan, Pat?" DJ asked. "Youngstown and Cleveland PD are working hard to find this first killer. That will give us a lot of answers," the cop replied. "For the public and media we are sticking with the story of one serial killer."

"So what should we be doing?" DJ asked. "Four things," O'Malley responded. "First we want you to go through all your footage of the Gardens again and note any little thing that seems out of the ordinary. I mean any little thing. It could be important. Second, we want you to continue to do your work in the Gardens while being on the lookout for anything unusual. And third... not a word of any of this to anyone. No social media, no conversations with anyone, nothing."

"Uh, Pat," Ren prodded "That's only three." "I know," the officer replied. "But I don't want to mention the fourth now." "Why not?" Peggy asked. "Because it could put you in a lot of danger."

CHAPTER 22

"Danger?" Peggy echoed "What do you mean danger?" "I don't want to say anything yet," O'Malley replied. "The Captain and I have been arguing about, er, discussing a possible plan that would involve you three. But don't worry about it. Just go do those other three things we spoke about… and be careful!"

The three left the room and as soon as they got outside all three started talking at once about what the dangerous plan might be. As they got into the car, DJ suggested they take the officer's advice and go about their business. First they needed to check in with their client.

Dr. Raselok was encouraging. He was eager to get the gardens on MLK finished so they could complete the East Blvd gardens next and start editing the project. "It would be great to have something to show the media and public by One World Day," he reminded them. "We will do our best, Doc," Ren replied and the three started making their plans for the next day's work.

It was a sunny morning which was not the best for photos and videos but made it pleasant to be in the Gardens. They started in the Finnish Garden which was just north of the India Garden on the west side of MLK. The largest Finnish community in Cleveland lived a little east of the city in a suburb called Fairport Harbor. That's the location of the Finnish Heritage Museum and a lot of other Finnish activities.

The Finnish Garden includes a bust honoring Johan Ludvig

Runeberg, the National Poet of Finland and author of the Finnish national anthem, "Maame." They also honor Elias Lonnrot, a Finnish physician and folklorist. There is a granite monument and quote from Finnish author Alexsis Kivi and busts of Jean Sibelius, noted composer of "Finlandia", and Finnish Statesman and Philosopher Johan Vilhelm Snellman.

On One World Day the community representatives display a large placard showing the Angry Bird character. Peggy had pointed out that Angry Birds was created in Finland.

They also teach a few phrases in Finnish including a word that became a favorite of DJ. "Sisu" is a word that doesn't directly translate to English but the idea is of courage, fortitude, stick-to-it-iveness. Sisu has been described as "the word that explains Finland."

Many visitors to the Finnish Garden ask about neighboring countries and Ken and the other Finns patiently explain that the Scandinavian countries are Sweden, Norway, Denmark and Iceland while Finland is geographically close but not the same. In fact, the Finnish language is closer to Hungarian then Swedish.

It's a smaller garden then some and the trio finished their chronicling of the Finnish Garden pretty fast. They moved a little north on MLK staying on the west side of the street and entered the Estonian Garden. The Estonian community is probably even smaller than the Finnish population in Cleveland but they are a proud and active community. Estonia is one of the three Baltic nations along with Lithuania and Latvia.

The main feature of the Estonian Garden is the symbolic flame to Estonia established in 1966 when Estonia was still a state within the USSR. The inscribed flame represents freedom from bondage, and hope for a brighter future.

The inscription on the monument is from Kalevipoeg, an epic poem written by Friedrich Reinhold Kreutzwald, a writer and physician. Part of the broader awakening of nationalist sentiment in Europe, Kalevipoeg became a lightning rod for the creation of Estonian national identity, of self-confidence and pride. It reads: "But the time will come when all torches will burst into flame at both ends."

In 2010 they completed the remodeling of the Estonian Garden's central area with a large, sandstone, boat-like planter surrounded by sandstone walks.

On One World Day they stream a large banner in the blue, black and white colors of the Estonian flag across the monument. Erika, the Gardens Federation rep for the Estonian Garden, was doing some flower pruning as the three approached. "Good morning Erika," they all greeted. "Where's Aavo?"

Aavo is Erika's husband and usual companion when working in the garden. With the recent murders they were concerned about Erika being there all alone.

"Good morning kids," Erika replied "Aavo is up at the coffee shop getting us some fortification. Do you want some? I can call him on his cell." "No thanks, we're good," they replied.

Erika was a sweetheart but she had an inner strength. She and her family were taken from their home in Estonia and placed in DP camps by the Russians. There were a lot of hardships and DJ was always impressed by how she kept such a cheerful and sunny disposition after what she had been through.

They did their work in the Estonian Garden and lingered a little longer than they might have hoping that Aavo would return so Erika would not be alone. In a few minutes he came driving up and was surprised to see the group. "I would have brought coffee for all if I knew we were having a party," he quipped. "I got the coffee and went to get gas and then stopped at the bank and… you know how it is."

The three were relieved that the couple were reunited and they said their goodbyes and moved north to the Latvian Garden.

Like the Estonians, the Latvian community was relatively small but active. The Latvian Garden was dedicated in 2006. The President of Latvia visited the Garden a few years ago and was visibly impressed by seeing his homeland remembered and showcased thousands of miles away in Cleveland, Ohio. Latvian Garden reps Anda, Ilze and their community were rightfully proud.

Two granite benches reminiscent of a boat and a "stream" rock symbolize the many rivers, lakes, and the Baltic Sea in Latvia. Another rock sculpture has an inscription and is encircled with a traditional Latvian "namejs" design which is recognizable to all Latvians and is one of the popular designs used in Latvian jewelry.

Peggy pointed out the Birch trees in the Garden and said they are prevalent in Latvia's landscape and poetry. The focal point of the

Latvian Cultural Garden is the arched stone sculpture in the center. The sculpture is a granite boulder from Latvia. The center arch represents the passage of immigrants from Latvia to the United States. The silhouette is of a woman in traditional folk dress and signifies the strength and spirit of the Latvian people. It was a magnet for photos as everyone wanted to appear inside the stone cutout. This included Peggy who inserted herself in the sculpture and asked the others to take her picture.

They complied and Peggy vogued a little for a few shots and then her eyes widened and her face turned ashen.

"Oh no!" she cried.

CHAPTER 23

The guys followed Peggy's gaze toward the Latvian rock in the southwest corner of the garden. They soon had the same wan complexion after moving closer and surveying the scene. It was Angel Annie lying crumpled behind the stone with blood pooling around her head.

They rushed to her but could tell it was too late for any medical attention. Peggy dropped to her knees to attempt CPR anyway but DJ and Ren held her back. "She's gone, Peggy." DJ cried. "We can't help her and there may be clues so we can't touch her." Peggy pulled away, walked a few feet and threw up. DJ and Ren felt the same.

They had all seen the napkin from the Cultural Gardens Coffee Shop with the terrible phrase "You don't belong here." "We better call O'Malley," DJ mumbled. Ren said "Wait, I have a better idea. I saw him making the rounds not too long ago by the Azerbaijan Garden. Let me go tell him in person to keep it off the 911 scanners and away from Katrina DeSanto and others." Ren hopped on his hoverboard and soon was cruising down MLK.

Meanwhile, DJ started taking photos and videos of the scene as Peggy sobbed near the body of their friend. Out of the corner of his eye DJ thought he saw movement in the next garden, the Ukrainian Garden. He blinked back the tears to look closer and saw the figure of Carl Jefferson moving quickly past the mammoth statue of Lesla Ukrainka and heading north.

DJ's mind raced. What was Carl doing there? He rarely ventured out of the African-American Garden except to argue with Ernie. DJ adjusted the focus and shot some video of the figure before it got too far away.

Soon Officer O'Malley pulled up, sans lights and siren, and Reckless Ren was not too far behind on his hoverboard. "Good idea trying to keep this quiet," the cop said. "I texted Captain Davenport and hopefully we will stall the media for a while by not using the police radio frequencies."

As if on cue, the Captain's car pulled up in front of the garden. He did not look happy. "Why is it that you three are always around trouble?" he grumbled as he proceeded to the crime scene.

"Did you touch anything?" he growled. "Peggy held Annie's head to see if she was OK and hugged her but other than that all we did was start documenting the scene with photos and videos," DJ answered. The five gathered around the lifeless body of Angel Annie and it was obvious that the manner of death was the same as the others. Not to mention the telltale note on the napkin.

Captain Davenport nodded. His usual stern countenance seemed to have softened and he looked genuinely sad. The brutal death of the harmless soul had gotten to him. In a minute he stiffened and his mind seemed to clear. He was all business again. "O'Malley," he barked "Once I call the medical examiner and the crime scene unit all hell will break lose and the media will show up. Is there anything we need to do before I make that call?"

They circled the crime scene and mumbled a few phrases to each other before the Captain grabbed his radio and made the call. "This is not going to be good," he predicted.

Within minutes two more Cleveland PD squad cars arrived and they were closely followed by a forensics unit and the medical examiner. DJ, Ren and Peggy stayed out of the way but observed and documented everything they could, just in case.

It was just 10 minutes later that a Cleveland Press car pulled up and Katrina DeSanto hopped out. This was quickly followed by news vans from three of the local TV stations. This had become the biggest story in town. The reporters were jockeying for shots and bombarding the Captain with questions. "Who was the victim? Is it the same serial killer? Any clues? Any witnesses? Are people safe in the Cultural Gardens?" And so on.

They became silent as the Captain began to speak. "This is currently an active crime scene. You are not to cross the yellow crime scene tape. We will have an official statement at a press conference this afternoon. My office will notify you of the time."

"That's not good enough!" a voice bellowed approaching from the street. It was Reginald Wilson with Theodore Mudhedge and his usual cadre of hangers-on and lackeys in tow. All eyes turned to the real estate developer and the reporters and cameras moved as one toward him. Ren whispered to DJ, "How did he get here so soon? I bet DeSanto is tipping him off."

Reginald Wilson continued. "How many more people have to die before the city shuts down this cesspool of crime? The police can't protect the public yet they want families to come here and be targets. And they are helping to encourage tens of thousands to come down here for what they call One World Day. That kind of crowd will be like shooting fish in a barrel for the killer and any other criminals that may be hanging out in this godforsaken "garden'."

The camera crews were rolling and DeSanto was writing furiously even as she held out her voice recorder.

"I call on the mayor and the Chief of Police," Wilson continued glancing over at a very unhappy Captain Davenport, "to close this dangerous area to the public. My plan will not only keep our precious citizens safe from serial killers but also bring jobs and prosperity to this area." He went on for another 10 minutes and DJ noticed Katrina DeSanto nodding her head vigorously as the businessman spoke. That was a sure sign of the slant her article in the Press would take.

When the impromptu speech finished, the crowd dispersed and DJ sidled up to Officer O'Malley. He whispered, "Pat, I think we may have a clue. And I do not like what it might tell us."

CHAPTER 24

The police officer grabbed DJ's arm and led him across the street to the Hungarian Garden for privacy. "What have you got?" he demanded. Before DJ could answer Ernie appeared. He had been working in the Garden and approached the pair. "O'Malley," he barked, "What are you doing to catch this murderer? A lot of my friends at the Hungarian Hall are afraid to come down here anymore. They managed to escape the communists in 1956 only to be afraid for their life in a peaceful garden? It's not right. They are starting to agree with that weasel Wilson. We've been here for over 100 years and I won't allow that. It's bad enough they changed the street name from Liberty Blvd. but they can't close down the gardens."

"We are working hard, Ernie," O'Malley responded. "Maybe you can help us. Did you notice anything unusual across the street in the last 24 hours or so?"

"Yeah," Ernie replied. "I noticed those 3 kids taking pictures and then I noticed you and your Captain showing up and the whole hullabaloo. I noticed it all."

"Nothing out of the ordinary before the three showed up?" Pat asked resignedly.

"Now I have to do your job for you too?" Ernie growled and spun around and headed back to his pruning.

O'Malley sighed. "OK DJ what did you have to tell me?"

As DJ started to speak he was interrupted by Ernie who shouted across the garden "Hey O'Malley. I did notice something."

Ernie strode back over to the two after carefully placing his pruning shears down. "There was something out of the ordinary."

"What?" O'Malley asked expectantly.

"I don't know if it's important," Ernie hemmed and hawed. "Maybe it's not important."

"What?" O'Malley repeated. "Any little thing may help us."

"Okay," Ernie replied, seeming hesitant to continue. "I've been pruning and weeding since early this morning and I noticed that before the kids got there someone else was near the garden. Someone I've never seen in that garden before."

"Can you describe the person?" The officer asked. "Sure," Ernie replied "But why don't I just tell you who it was?"

"Who?" O'Malley ejaculated with growing exasperation.

"It was Carl Jefferson from the African American Garden. I rarely see him this far south on the street if there's not an event or if he's not bothering me with his misguided opinions."

O'Malley stopped writing in his notebook. "Carl?" he asked "Are you sure?"

Of course I'm sure," Ernie huffed. "I may be old but I'm not blind."

"What was he doing?" Pat asked. "I saw him walking toward the Latvian Garden and then later I noticed him moving pretty fast north toward the Ukrainian Garden."

The police officer coaxed as many details as he could out of Ernie and then thanked him and started walking away with DJ.

"I know Ernie and Carl aren't best friends," he said "but to make something up like that is out of character."

DJ paused and then said, "He wasn't making it up. We saw Carl too."

"That's what I wanted to tell you," DJ continued. Peggy and I saw a figure moving pretty fast from the Latvian Garden through the Ukrainian Garden and when we zoomed in we saw that it was Carl."

O'Malley paused. "Have you told anyone else this?" DJ shook his head "no." "Don't," O'Malley ordered. "I can't believe Carl has anything to do with this but we have to talk to him. He is now a person of interest."

"What's going to happen with Angel Annie?" DJ asked after

reflecting for a minute. "The medical examiner and crime scenes scientists will do their investigation and make their report," O'Malley answered. "Then I guess her body will go the county morgue. As far as we know she doesn't have any family."

"Don't let her go to the county." DJ replied. "Let us see if we can figure something out so she gets a proper funeral and burial. She deserves it. We will be her next of kin if nobody else can be found."

O'Malley nodded. "I want to be involved too," he said.

The news and social media were full of the latest killing and the speech by Reginald Wilson. Radio talk shows were dedicated to opinions on the situation. Theodore Mudhedge was making the rounds of the TV stations pleading his boss's case. Social media was buzzing.

Popular opinion seemed to be shifting. At first it seemed like a few unfortunate crimes that just happen to occur in any big city. Now people were blaming the Cultural Gardens and calling it a dangerous place. Katrina DeSanto's column and editorials in the Cleveland Press were leaning toward the plan to close the Gardens and sell them to Wilson for development.

The Mayor was stopped on his way to a city council meeting and grilled on the failure to bring the killer to justice and protect the community. Several city council members were gauging the shifting popular opinion and starting to speak out in favor of the sale to Wilson. The Mayor then contacted the Police Chief and Captain Davenport and chewed them both out. Tempers were starting to flare.

Several city council members grandstanded at the meeting that evening and called for the firing of the Chief of Police. In the public forum part of the meeting, none other than Reginald Wilson approached the microphone. With Mudhedge's help he whipped the audience, triple the size of a normal city council meeting, into a frenzy with his speech. The media ate it up and it was the lead story on the evening news.

Wilson told the council that in the absence of leadership from the Mayor's office, they needed to step in and make the citizens of Cleveland safe. He promoted his upcoming public rally to demand that those in charge be held accountable and the Gardens closed and made safe. Many of the city council members nodded their heads in agreement. They would be there to share in the limelight. It was good politics after all. Who isn't in favor of public safety and economic development?

DJ, Ren and Peggy tried to stay away from social media and in the words of Captain Davenport "Just keep the hell quiet." They were going over their latest pictures and videos when the phone rang. It was their client Dr. Raselok. Ren put them on speaker and asked "What's up Doc?"

The professor's voice was shaky as he said, "We need to end the Cultural Gardens project."

CHAPTER 25

The three were silent. This was their only paying gig. It was the project that was going to take their fledgling startup business to the next level. Plus they all really loved the Cultural Gardens and what they represented. They didn't want Dr. Raselok to know but they would have done this project for free.

"Hello? Hello?" the speaker buzzed. "Are we still connected?" the prof asked. DJ cleared his throat and replied "Yes Doc. Why do you want to end the project?"

The Professor pointed out the murders and how he was afraid for the safety of DJ, Ren and Peggy. "I don't want anything to happen to you three because of this project. It's become too dangerous. It looks like Wilson will get his way and the Cultural Gardens will be no more anyway."

All three spoke at once and then stopped. DJ conveyed the feelings of the group. "We really don't want to stop Doc. This is an important project and we really want to complete it. We are very careful and will continue to be so. Plus, Wilson hasn't won yet. There are still a lot of people who don't want to see the Cultural Gardens turned into a strip mall and parking lots. We need to fight this. Plus, we are almost done with capturing the content."

Raselok replied "I appreciate that but your safety has to come first. If you three promise to stick together, never go anywhere in the

Gardens alone and be extra careful we can give it a few more days. Please be careful and if at any time you don't feel safe and want to stop work just do it. I won't be mad or disappointed."

The professor continued "What about One World Day? That was going to be our big pre-promotion event. Do you think it will go on?"

DJ answered "Let's keep planning on it. Everyone we talk to from the Cleveland Cultural Gardens Federation is still on board, though the support of a few is wavering. I can't imagine them cancelling One World Day after over 75 years in a row. But, if Wilson can sway public opinion, and city council, they may force the Federation, Police and the Mayor to cancel it." He paused, "That would be a shame."

They worked on some more logistical plans for the project and the trio assured D. Raselok that they would be very careful but would be continuing with their work – but at a faster pace.

The plan was to finish off the gardens on MLK and the hill between MLK and East Boulevards. Instead of their usual approach – DJ, Ren and Peggy going their separate directions and doing their thing on their own - the group decided to fulfill their promise to their sponsor and stick together. The Ukrainian Garden, where they had spotted the figure of Carl hustling away from the site of Angel Annie's murder, was next on the list.

The main attraction was a tall statue of the poet Larysa Petrivna Kosach-Kvitka better known by her pseudonym, Lesya Ukrainka. She was one of Ukraine's best-known poets and writers and the foremost woman writer in Ukrainian literature. Her statue was rededicated in a ceremony on One World Day 2011 on her 140th birthday.

The Ukrainian Garden was inaugurated in 1940 and is composed of a series of brick and stone courts connected by paved walks. Three bronze busts celebrate significant nationalist leaders in Ukraine history: poet and writer Ivan Franko; Grand Prince of Kiev Volodymyr the Great; and Taras Hryhorovych Shevchenko, a poet, teacher and artist.

With all 3 concentrating on the Ukrainian garden, they finished the job quickly. The west side of MLK then had a little gap before getting to the African-American garden and then another gap before the Romanian Garden.

They packed their gear and headed north toward the African-American Garden. As they approached, they could see Carl and a few of his volunteers with rakes and other tools.

Peggy asked, "Should we talk to Carl about what we saw?" "Let's play it by ear," Ren answered "but I think we should see what he has to say. But be careful. He could be the murderer."

The African American Garden was on a wide space of land and included a large hill connecting the lower level with the street level above. Up top was where Phase I of the garden was completed. The design by architect Daniel W. Bickerstaff conveys the past, present and future of the African American community.

The concept of the Past Pavilion, the first installation in the garden, is to translate the experience of the Trans-Atlantic Slave Trade through a reinterpretation of the corridors and dungeons and the "door of no return" in the slave castles along the western coast of Africa.

The pavilion depicts stages of the slave passage to the new world with its polished black granite sculptural walls which create a sensation of compression, tension and apprehension. The Door of No Return is the sandstone portal addressing the notion of unknown transition. The Infinity Fountain echoes the illusion of the tranquility of the Atlantic Ocean as seen through the actual Doorway of No Return.

The future plans for the garden include a continuance of the journey down the hill to the MLK level.

"Well, if it isn't the Mod Squad," Carl bellowed as he saw the three approaching? Their blank stares prompted him to chuckle and add "I guess I'm showing my age."

Ren was already checking his phone and reported that The Mod Squad was a late-60's early 70's TV show that featured "the hippest and first young undercover cops on TV …One black, one white, one blonde".

He read on until Peggy interrupted "But I'm not blonde and I'm certainly not a hippie." Ren chimed in "And I'm Asian, not African American." DJ was looking at the web images and added "I sure didn't come from a wealthy home in Beverly Hills."

Carl sighed. "OK, OK it was just an observation not a description. What are you three up to? Feel free to grab a rake and get to work."

They explained that they were continuing their work chronicling the Gardens for their project. "Great idea," Carl said. "The story of these Gardens is the story of Cleveland and the story of America." He went on and on with a speech that could have been delivered by his supposed nemesis Ernie. After providing details on the history of the African-American Garden, Carl eventually paused and took a breath.

Ren took the opportunity to jump in and said "Since you brought up the Mod Squad… We were wondering what you knew about Angel Annie's murder or any of the other crimes."

Carl seemed taken aback. "Why would I know anything?" he asked warily. Peggy answered "Well, you are in the Gardens as much as anyone besides maybe Ernie. Have you seen or heard anything?"

"Ernie? That old goat," Carl erupted. "I do twice the work in our Garden as he does in his. Did he say something about me? I'm going to have to have a little talk with him I guess."

They assured him that Ernie was not talking about him and explained that they were just wondering if he had any ideas on the crimes. "Not really," he offered. "When I first heard about the message on the note I was convinced that it was racially motivated. When someone says 'You don't belong here' to a black person that's what it usually means. But Angel Annie's explanation made sense." He seemed to choke up when he mentioned the name of the latest victim.

Carl added "I am broken hearted about Annie. She really was an Angel. What kind of monster would do that to such a kind and innocent soul?"

The foursome was quiet as they all reflected on their own experiences with the gentle homeless woman. Blinking his moist eyes Ren snapped out of it and blurted "So what were you doing running away from the crime scene?"

CHAPTER 26

"What are you talking about," Carl growled. DJ explained how they had been in the Latvian Garden and discovered the body and then saw Carl running away in the Ukrainian Garden.

Carl was incensed. "You sure are nothing like the Mod Squad," he snorted. "Who do you think you are? Are you accusing me of murder? Did Ernie say something? After all the time we have spent together at One World Day and other events in the Gardens and you think I could do something like that? And to Angel Annie no less?"

He went on like that for another few minutes before DJ interrupted. "Carl, we know that you are not the killer and never could be, but we know what we saw and even more, we have it on video."

Carl paused. "So it was you. I was wondering why O'Malley was grilling me about my whereabouts yesterday. I can't believe you kids would narc on me."

"We didn't narc," Ren objected "We just shared our content with the police in hopes of bringing justice to the murderer of Angel Annie and the others. We have to stop this guy for their sake and for potential future victims."

"We can't let him scare people away from the Cultural Gardens and One World Day," Peggy chimed in.

"Or her," Carl added.

"What?" Peggy replied. "Or her," he answered "Maybe the killer is a woman. You just said 'him' like you always do. In fact, it's interesting that you always seem to be in the middle of these murders Peggy. Do you have an alibi?"

Peggy's mouth flew open and she was about to protest when Carl grinned and held up his hand. "Doesn't feel so good to be accused, does it? Now close your mouth young lady. It's not becoming."

DJ and Ren looked over at Peggy whose mouth was still agape and burst into laughter.

"So, what were you doing there Carl?" DJ asked after the laughter died down. "It's none of your business young man. That's what I told the police too."

The three looked down, each wondering to themselves if Carl could have something to hide. "If you can keep a secret I'll tell you. You're good kids but you sure are nosy."

Carl leaned close and in a hushed whisper began "As my wife has pointed out repeatedly, I might have put on a few pounds over the last few years. I blame her cooking. So I decided to try some of the things I learned in the Service when I was in the best shape of my life."

He paused and looked around and then continued. "I started doing some calisthenics and a little jogging. But I sure am not going to give her the satisfaction of thinking she was right so I have been doing my exercise up the road a little where I thought nobody would see me. Turns out everybody saw me – you kids for starters."

The trio looked sheepish but all were relieved at the plausible explanation. They hoped the police would be satisfied with Carl's story.

"I did you kids a solid now do something for me," he asked. "Find the punk who killed Angel Annie and the others and stop that crook Reginald Wilson from shutting down our Gardens!"

They hugged Carl, assured him they would and headed back to work.

Right next to the African American Garden was the Romanian Garden and after a quick break the trio worked on documenting it. The Romanian Cultural Garden was dedicated in 1967. Along with an Ohio Historical Marker telling about the United Romanian Societies and Carpatina there is a statue of Romanian composer, violin virtuoso and conductor George Enescu up the hill in the large green garden.

They rushed over to the Azerbaijan Garden and continued working. The Azerbaijan Cultural Garden was dedicated in May 2008. It was on the east side of MLK Boulevard and featured the "Hearth" sculpture, a rounded funnel structure made of eight tons of highly polished stainless steel.

The installation is the creation of an Azerbaijani artist. A stone flanks the large bowl-shaped sculpture. The inscription etched into its stone says: "Azerbaijan - land of eternal fire, ignites the imagination, warms the spirit and kindles the soul."

The trio had heard that a wealthy person from Azerbaijan was recuperating in the Cleveland Clinic, heard about the Cultural Gardens and spearheaded the project.

Finishing quickly, they packed up their gear and headed back to the studio to check and begin processing their work. The mood was lighter than it had been as they were making progress on their project and, more importantly, no gruesome discoveries had been made.

All three instinctively checked their phones and were shocked to see the breaking news headline: "Cultural Gardens Murderer Caught!"

CHAPTER 27

They jumped up and down and hugged celebrating the great news. "Finally!" Peggy exulted. "The Cultural Gardens are again a safe place of peace through mutual understanding." "I wonder who it was." Ren asked. "I wonder why he did it." "Or she," DJ added, remembering Carl's earlier admonishment. While interested in the particulars, the three were content to enjoy the sudden relief without pursuing all the details of the arrest just yet. The four murders were still a terrible and sad tragedy, especially losing their friend Angel Annie, but with the murderer caught the killing would end. And so would the threat of cancelling One World Day and the terrible plans by Reginald Wilson to buy up the Gardens.

The Cleveland Cultural Gardens project was going to be the showpiece of their new company's portfolio. The three had very different talents and skills but a complementary vision so it seemed like a perfect combination. They had already been discussing future undertakings once they had a successful launch of the Cultural Gardens project. Recommendations and referrals from someone as well-connected and distinguished as Dr. Raselok would lead to other paying projects they hoped.

The day's coverage was downloaded and reviewed and all three were very happy with the results. They were on a roll.

They ordered some dinner from one of their favorite AsiaTown restaurants, Li Wah. DJ suggested "Let's agree not to check our phones or social media while we eat. We need a break." Ren agreed and said "Hey, why don't we watch some episodes of that TV show that Carl talked about – the Mob Squad." "Not Mob Squad," Peggy corrected "It's Mod Squad."

"Mob, Mod, whatever. Let's do it," Ren replied and dug into the Pad Thai as DJ searched for Season 1 of the Mod Squad. They settled in, plates full and TV cued when the good feeling was interrupted by a call with the ringtone indicating it was from Officer O'Malley.

"So close," DJ muttered as he reluctantly answered the phone. "He must want to tell us the good news."

Unfortunately, it was not what they had expected and hoped for. DJ put his phone on speaker and the three offered greetings to the officer.

"Sounds like congratulations are in order," DJ announced. "For what?" O'Malley responded. "For solving the case, for catching the serial killer. We saw the breaking news headline."

There was a pause and then Officer O'Malley started to explain. "We did make an arrest. We have in custody one Otis Miller who has been charged with the murder of the first victim Valarie Wills and other charges. Miller was holed up in a Toledo apartment and was arrested on a drug charge there. When his fingerprints and DNA were identified we knew he was our killer and they transferred him to Cleveland."

"That's great. Congratulations," Peggy jumped in. "Did he say why he killed Angel Annie and the others?" "That's just it," responded O'Malley. "He didn't kill the others. He just killed the first victim. Our theory was right. He killed his ex in Youngstown and dumped the body in his old stomping grounds in the Hungarian Cultural Garden. He then took off and has been on the run ever since, nowhere near the Gardens or Cleveland."

"So the serial killer really is a copycat and is still out there?" Ren asked resignedly. "I'm afraid so," O'Malley answered.

"Well, thanks for calling and letting us know," DJ said and began to hang up. "Wait!" Officer O'Malley barked "That's not why I called. Have you seen it yet? We have more problems."

O'Malley told them to check social media for the latest. Reginald Wilson must have spent a fortune because his postings scaring people away from the Gardens and toward his plan were everywhere. He was buying links, likes, favorites and retweets.

The accounts of Theodore Mudhedge, Katrina DeSanto and several others whom they had never heard of were similarly blowing up. It was an all-out social media blitz.

"Money talks," Ren grumbled. "We can't counter all those paid placements with our own postings."

The three scrolled through page after page of posts from Wilson and his minions. "What can we do, Pat?" DJ inquired. "I'm afraid it's time to go to the fourth part of the plan," Officer O'Malley answered with reluctance. "The dangerous part."

The three went to the police station early the next day. They never did watch the Mod Squad the night before, or even finish their dinners. None of the three would ever imagine that they would leave delicious shumai dumplings uneaten. The anticipation of what this dangerous plan might be had changed the mood and they all went home and had restless nights.

Sipping two coffees and one "Peggy" the three sat in silence as Officer O'Malley and then Captain Davenport entered the room. The Captain did not look happy but it was a different expression from his usual angry face.

Captain Davenport looked like he hadn't slept in a week. He sat down and looked the three over. "I hope you understand the gravity of the situation," he began. "If it wasn't so serious I wouldn't even consider asking what I am going to ask you. In fact, I still can't believe that I am going to do this. And I won't blame you if you don't want to do it."

Davenport paused and looked like he was fighting some inner turmoil. Officer O'Malley continued for him. "This has become much larger than just the 4 terrible murders. We don't want to dismiss those tragedies in any way but in addition to that there is an organized and well-funded group calling for the recall of the Mayor and Police Chief, not to mention Captain Davenport."

"Even more, this group, led by Reginald Wilson as you know, is getting close to having City Council approve his plan to buy the Cultural Gardens. With his spending in both traditional and social media he is swaying public opinion to his side. Did you see his full-page ad in the Cleveland Press today? It is a real possibility that the Cleveland Cultural Gardens will soon be sold to that profiteering land baron."

"Damn it," Davenport pounded the table. "I grew up in this neighborhood. The Cultural Gardens are important to the people – all the people – of Cleveland and they also send a message to the world. I can't allow them to be destroyed even if it means asking you to do something dangerous."

When the Captain pounded the table Ren and DJ squeezed their coffee cups till they spilled over and Peggy looked as green as her healthy namesake drink.

"What do you want us to do?" DJ asked in a voice he didn't recognize. He cleared his throat and repeated the question.

It seemed like hours before the Captain answered.

CHAPTER 28

When they left the police station they each used their individual social media accounts, and the combined company accounts, to tease their followers on the upcoming project. They retweeted, liked and favorited more than ever before.

They also promoted the upcoming One World Day, assuring their followers that the City, Cleveland Cultural Gardens Federation and the other powers that be would not let such an important and historic event be cancelled.

Their social media barrage continued as they worked in the Gardens that day. They were nearing the end of their project and were eager to complete it and sit down with Dr. Raselok and start promoting it.

They let all their followers know that they would be finishing the Gardens on the north end of MLK, nearest Lake Erie. There weren't any monuments in the proposed Native American, Korean or Vietnamese Gardens yet but the trio documented the foliage and landscape.

They were excited about the prospects of the new gardens and wondered what the Native American and Korean communities might be planning.

The Vietnamese community was the furthest along with their plans of the three. Gia Hoa had left Vietnam in the 70's and along with Joe, a Vietnam Veteran, they were the leaders of the Vietnamese Cultural Garden committee. Their plans were for a large statue of a Vietnamese woman in the center of the garden in a field of bamboo.

The Armenian Garden Designed by architect Berj A. Shakarian, assumes the form of the "vesica piscis", a sacred geometric symbol representing Christ, and by extension, the conversion of Armenia as the first Christian nation in 301 CE. The Alphabet Monument is the central symbol and is composed of staggered granite blocks, representing both the turbulent history of the Armenian people and the ruggedly beautiful landscape of Armenia and the Caucasus Mountains. Peggy told them that St. Mesrop Mashtots invented the alphabet circa 404 CE in order to translate the Bible into the Armenian language.

The three kept live streaming and posting about their progress. Thousands were seeing their posts about which garden they were in. They crossed the street to the new Russian Garden next. The formal dedication of the Russian Cultural Garden was held in September, 2018.

Russian reps Svetlana and Boris have big plans for the Russian Garden but the first phase of the Garden that was featured at the dedication was a series of inscribed stones called the Walk of Fame. The first ring of the Walk of Fame honors Russian cultural and scientific heroes such as Leo Tolstoy, Aleksandr Solzhenitsyn, Dmitri Shostakovich, Vladimir Nabokov and numerous Nobel Prize winners. The first bust was of Yuri Gagarin, the first human in space.

The last (most Northern) garden on MLK Blvd. is the Albanian Garden. After posting their intentions to conclude the day's work at the Albanian Garden the three grabbed their gear and headed north.

Dedicated in 2012, the first phase of the Albanian Cultural Garden features a statue of the beloved humanitarian and sister to the poor, Mother Teresa. Many associate Mother Teresa with India but she was of Albanian heritage and born in Skopje. The piece was created by noted Albanian sculptor Kreshnik Xhiku.

The three had to take selfies with the large statue of the saint and they were in awe that one end of the Cultural Gardens was anchored by Mother Teresa while Mahatma Gandhi stood watch at the other end. How had such a place of peace and diversity become so dangerous?

When they arrived at the office to download and process that day's content they noticed a voicemail from Dr. Raselok. They reached him as he was driving home from work and he congratulated them on their day's efforts.

"Wow!" he exclaimed "You guys were all over the web today.

Every time I looked there were postings from at least one of you. That will make our job promoting the project a lot easier. Way to create a buzz!"

"Thanks Doc," DJ replied. "We are going to hit it hard tomorrow again and may actually finish the filming and photos. If not, the next day for sure."

"What are you covering first?" the professor asked. "Well, we have to cover the northern end of East Blvd. and a few gardens we missed," said DJ "so we will either start north at the Polish Garden or more south by the Greek. It depends on how the sun and clouds are for filming."

"Well keep up the good work and be careful out there. If Reginald Wilson gets his way this project may be the only complete documentation of the Gardens. Future generations will rely on your work."

"Speaking of Wilson," Raselok continued "Do the police think he may be involved in the murders? I wouldn't put it past him to have Mudhedge kill people so they can make some money."

"Speak of the devil," Ren interrupted. "Officer O'Malley is pulling up right now. Talk to you later Doc."

Pat O'Malley opened the door and held out a bag of bagels. "I come bearing gifts," he exclaimed. They all dug in and while DJ and Ren were spreading cream cheese on their second bagel, Peggy asked "So is this just a social call Pat?"

"Yes and no," the cop hedged. "It's not official police business but I want to discuss the case with you. Let's talk this thing through and see what we can come up with. Who could be behind the murders?"

The ideas flowed. Is it possible that Carl wasn't really jogging that day when they saw him leave Angel Annie's murder scene? Could Ernie be mad enough at some of the newcomers to the Gardens to try and scare them off with murder?

They all agreed that it had to be someone who knew the Gardens well enough to be able to commit the act and then get away without being seen. Did one of the regular workers – Paul, Lex, Tom, Char or one of the others – have some unknown issue that would drive them to kill?

Or was it some random psycho or evil person that had no real connection to the Gardens beyond their proximity to where he or she lived or worked?

O'Malley said "In my 35 years as a cop I've learned to look at who profits from a crime to figure out who did it. So who profits from the murders and terror in the Cultural Gardens?"

DJ answered, "Certainly, Reginald Wilson does. If people are afraid to visit the Gardens, the City will sell him the land and let him build his condos and shopping malls. Not to mention his lackey, that weasel Theodore Mudhedge. I wouldn't put anything past him."

"Katrina DeSanto is certainly doing well for herself," Peggy added. She is on the national and cable news networks every night and I hear she has been offered a position with the Associated Press. With every murder in the Gardens, her career takes off some more."

The ideas and conversation continued along those lines as the last crumbs of bagel were devoured. Traversing all that territory had given their appetites a boost.

As they were wrapping up, Officer O'Malley got serious and said "You know you don't have to continue with the plan. If you feel uneasy or scared you don't have to do it."

"We can handle it," Ren replied. "We are ready to go full force with it tomorrow and yes, before you say it Pat, we will be very careful."

CHAPTER 29

Armed with 2 coffees and a 'Peggy" from the Cultural Gardens Coffee Shop the trio started the day's work on the corner of East Boulevard and St. Clair in the Polish Garden. They used their social media accounts to advertise their location and plans before heading over.

One of the best features of the Cleveland Cultural Gardens was the location of some of the gardens. Countries that may have current or historical differences or even wars might have their cultural garden near one another. All part of the "peace through mutual understanding."

The Turkish Garden was around the corner from the Armenian Garden and nobody batted an eye. Irish was near British, Indian near Pakistani, Hebrew near Syrian, Russian near Ukraine and so on. Maybe the real world couldn't get along but in the Cleveland Cultural Gardens they were able to.

The Polish Cultural Garden was dedicated in 1934. At the center of the garden is an octagonal fountain built largely by the help of small donations from schoolchildren and dedicated in 1953.

Surrounding the central fountain are busts showing famous Polish figures: Nicolaus Copernicus, Henryk Sienkiewicz, Frédéric Chopin, Madame Marie Sklodowska Curie, Ignacy Jan Paderewski and Adam Mickiewicz. In 2018, an impressive new bust of Saint Pope John Paul II was added.

The next garden was the Slovenian, originally named the Yugoslav Cultural Garden. It's been said that there are more Slovenians in Cleveland than anywhere in the world outside of Slovenia so it was no surprise when over 100,000 people paraded in support of the

Yugoslav Garden's dedication in 1938.

Originally the Yugoslav Garden shared the culture of Cleveland's Croatians, Serbians, and Slovenians but when the country of Yugoslavia dissolved in the 1980s and 1990s, three separate gardens emerged with the original space renamed the Slovenian Garden. The upper level contains a circular fountain and the busts of Bishop Frederick Barago, a missionary to the Ottawa and Ojibway Native American tribes and the first Slovenian Bishop in the US; Ivan Cankar, a poet and political activist and Ivan Zorman, a poet and composer. Also a relief in the wall of Simon Gregorcic a Slovene poet and Roman Catholic priest.

Making quick work of the garden the three started toward the Czech Garden when a voice called to them "Stop right there!"

They turned and saw the unpleasant visage of Reginald Wilson's right hand man, Theodore Mudhedge. He shuffled up to them and introduced himself.

"We know who you are Mudhedge and we are busy so... adios," Ren said and started to walk away. "Wait," Mudhedge countered "I have something you will be interested in."

That stopped the three and they took a few steps back to listen to what he had to say. "You know that Mr. Wilson is a man of great means," he began as the trio rolled their eyes. "You are smart people. You have to see that the politicians, the media and even public opinion have now turned to favor his proposal. He is continuing to fund advertising and his numerous public speeches are covered favorably by Katrina DeSanto and the Cleveland Press."

"Tell us something we don't know," grumbled Ren.

Mudhedge continued. "As I said, you are smart people. We have done our homework and we know you are trying to build and grow a business. Do you think being on the losing side of such a monumental change is in your interest or will reflect well on your fledgling company?"

Get to the point or we are walking," DJ butt in.

"Ok, OK. Mr. Wilson has granted me great latitude to convince you three to join the team. He is offering significant startup funds for your business, several sizeable contracts for projects and introductions to others needing your talents. His generous offer will insure that your startup becomes a successful early stage company poised for great growth and profit."

Mudhedge pulled out a checkbook and his left hand got busy filling it out. "Who should I make the first check out to?" he asked.

"Are you for real? Join the team? Does that mean what I think it does?" Peggy grimaced.

Mudhedge cleared his throat and made a face that did actually resemble a weasel. "Mr. Wilson is aware of your not insignificant social media presence and the trust that your followers have placed in you. He feels that if you three were to back his proposal that the deal would be complete within weeks if not sooner. You three would be substantially enriched, you would have a very powerful and wealthy friend in Mr. Wilson. And you may prevent another murder in the Gardens."

The distaste at the offer was overshadowed by that last line. "What do you mean prevent another murder? Is that a threat?" DJ asked. "What do you know about the killings?"

"Nothing, nothing more than what I read in the Press," he backpedaled. "But let's face it, the sooner the Gardens are sold to Mr. Wilson the sooner we can bring in our security teams and stop the murders."

The three turned away in disgust and DJ called back "You say you did your homework but you obviously don't know us very well. We would never sell our souls, or the Gardens, for money."

"Think about it," Mudhedge countered. "The offer is good for any of the three of you. Call me if you change your mind."

"I feel like I need a shower after listening to that slimy weasel," Peggy said as they trudged closer to the Czech Garden. 'Me too," DJ said. "Let's crank through the Czech Garden and then grab some lunch and talk about this."

The Czech Garden was dedicated in 1935. It is a big circle with an entrance monument on each side. They were greeted by Paul, the main caretaker of the Czech Garden, who kept the three informed and entertained as they processed the large space. Paul was a past-president of the Cleveland Cultural Gardens Federation and perhaps its most dedicated volunteer.

He pointed out the busts of Czech composer Antonin Dvorak, Czech historian and politician Frantisek Palacky, Czech painter Karel Havlícek and Jindrich Šimon Baar a Czech Catholic priest and writer.

In the middle of the garden is a full-size statue of "the father of modern education" Jan Amos Komensky. Another large statue in front of the wall honoring Czech immigrants is of the first president of Czechoslovakia, Tomas Masaryk. Paul told them how the nation of Czechoslovakia was initially formed with the Cleveland Agreement of 1915.

They asked Paul to join them for lunch but he wanted to continue his work in the garden. After a selfie with Paul the three diligently posted their location and plans for the next garden to their social media accounts.

"Well, well, well" a voice said. "Since when are you three so publicity conscious?"

CHAPTER 30

"What do you want Katrina?" Ren asked as they turned and saw the Cleveland Press reporter. "You three are obviously going out of your way to post your locations the last few days. What's going on?" she asked as she thrust a portable voice recorder at them and started writing in her notebook with her left hand.

"We saw how the irresponsible posts from people like you and Reginald Wilson are taking attention away from all the good in the Cultural Gardens," Peggy answered, "so we decided to post some positive things."

"Yeah, right," DeSanto snorted. "I know you are up to something and if I wasn't so busy with my new very lucrative assignments from several national media outlets I'd figure it out and expose you. But I have better things to do. Did I mention they are very lucrative assignments?"

"Gee, Katrina," Ren answered. "These murders sure seem to be making you happy. How do you sleep?"

Very well," she replied "and in a very expensive new bed. And soon I will be able to stuff my new mattress with cash when Reginald Wilson's plan comes to fruition."

"So much for the impartiality of the press," DJ grumbled. "If you don't mind, we have work to do so why don't you leave us alone."

"My pleasure," she said. "If you losers do anything interesting, I'll see it on social media anyway. Ta Ta." Ren grumbled "Since when does a girl from Collinwood say 'Ta Ta'?"

The three opened their backpacks but suddenly the sandwiches and pop didn't seem very appetizing. Even the chocolate chip cookies they had picked up earlier at the Cultural Gardens Coffee

Shop went untouched.

"Well it looks like Katrina DeSanto has sold out if not to Reginald Wilson at least to the tabloid media," Ren complained.

They sat in silence for a while and then DJ said quietly "I wouldn't blame either of you if you took Mudhedge's offer. It's looking bad for the Gardens so it may make sense for your future careers if..."

"Stop right there!" the other two interrupted. "We would never sell out the Gardens or the team for money," Peggy continued. "Never," Ren confirmed.

"Ok," DJ said with a big grin. "I thought so but just wanted to make sure. Let's continue with Captain Davenport's plan and save the Cultural Gardens!

Back at the studio they were relieved to catch up on the news and find out that no new problems had occurred. Sure there was a lot of noise from politicians and others for Wilson's plan but at least there weren't any murders.

They again made a point to publicize where they would be shooting the next day and then made a call to Officer O'Malley. "I guess no news is good news, right Pat?" DJ asked.

O'Malley agreed and said the plan was going as expected but the next few days would be the most dangerous. He urged the three to be extra careful before hanging up.

"Oh, one more thing," he added. "Forensics has confirmed that while the first murder was indeed committed by Otis Miller, the other three were committed by some other person - the same person. And while Miller is right-handed, the other murderer is a leftie. So be on the lookout for a southpaw."

The next day began with social media blasts telling the world exactly where they would be that morning. They started in the Rusin Garden and documented the focal point, a bust of Aleksander Duchnovich.

Rusyns don't have a country. They are an ethnic group who come from the Carpathian Mountains region bordering Ukraine, Slovakia and Poland. Peggy admitted that for years she thought the Rusin garden sign was a misspelling of Russian. She had never heard of the Rusyn people. DJ and Ren sheepishly fessed up too.

During the 1970's, the bust of Father Duchnovich disappeared from the garden. There was a lot of theft and vandalism in all the gardens then. John, a Carpatho-Rusyn Society member, worked hard to raise funds to replace the bust which was dedicated in a ceremony at the Rusin Garden in 2012.

Father Duchnovich was a priest, patriot, poet, educator and author of the Rusin National anthem. When offered his freedom from prison if he renounced his Rusin heritage, he said, "I was, am and always will be a Rusin." This saying is inscribed on the bust's pedestal.

"This is one of the reasons I love the Gardens," Peggy gushed. "I never would have known of this great man or this whole group of people." Ren and DJ made a face but inwardly they shared her sentiment.

Their social media blasts seemed to be working. Dozens of people had stopped by and greeted the three. Some took selfies with the trio and Peggy was asked out on several dates. Ren and DJ teased her unmercifully about this and she spent most of the morning blushing.

Ren had brought his hacky sack and drew small crowds as he kept the small object in the air. He regularly sent the sack flying toward people in the audience who caught it and then tossed it back.

DJ studied his friend for a few minutes before he caught on. Ren was checking for lefties! When he asked, Ren smiled and said, "Hey when there's a murderer out there I'll take any advantage I can!"

The three moved on, accompanied by a few hangers on, to the Slovak Garden. "I'm starting to feel like the Pied Piper," DJ said. "Have you noticed anyone suspicious?" Ren said there had been several lefties in the group so far but nothing jumped out to make them murder suspects.

Halfway there Peggy noticed she had left her water bottle behind and jogged back to retrieve it. DJ and Ren didn't notice she was missing as they laughed and took selfies with their new friends.

Peggy noticed her bottle behind the Duchnovich bust and bent to retrieve it. She was startled by a voice stating ominously, "You don't belong here."

Peggy screamed as she jerked up and saw Theodore Mudhedge and his smarmy smile looking at her. She started to run but tripped and fell. She tried to scramble to her feet but her body seemed frozen, like in a dream. Mudhedge came closer.

"Get away from me!" she screamed and kicked her legs out at the approaching threat. Mudhedge came closer looking more evil than weasel-like to Peggy. "What's the matter?" he oozed. "Are you afraid?"

He kept coming closer and with his left hand he pulled something out of his pocket and raised it. That's the last thing Peggy remembered as she lost consciousness.

CHAPTER 31

Peggy woke up with the smell of something terrible in her nose. The ammonia in the smelling salts had done their job and she was now wide awake. She noticed her glasses, with one lens cracked, were in her lap and put them on. She was sitting sideways in the back seat of Pat O'Malley's squad car.

DJ, Ren and the officer were all there and were obviously relieved and happy to see her awake. "What happened?" she managed to say in a shaky voice.

"You tell us first," O'Malley countered. "What do you remember? Why were you in the Rusin Garden with Mudhedge?"

Peggy shivered as she began to remember. She told how she had forgotten her water bottle and returned to retrieve it.

"Peggy you know we are not supposed to split up. What were you thinking?" Ren moaned.

DJ explained to her that they had been on their way to the Slovak Garden and were so preoccupied with their "entourage" that they didn't know Peggy has backtracked. When they heard a scream they ran toward its source.

"We saw you on the ground in the Rusin Garden with Theodore Mudhedge moving toward you," Ren chimed in. "DJ went all Cleveland Browns and made a diving tackle of that weasel. I went and checked on you. Pat pulled up in his squad car a few seconds after. And here we are."

Peggy was still shaken but was able to recount the details of her dealings with Mudhedge. "Is he the Cultural Gardens killer?" she asked. "Was I going to be the next victim?"

Officer O'Malley said "We have him in custody and will find that out soon. Right now you need to see a doctor to make sure you are OK. If you think of anything else, let me know."

She nodded and examined her glasses. Luckily she had a number of spare pairs at home. As DJ and Ren helped her out of the car and O'Malley sat in the driver's seat, Peggy had one more thought. "Pat, I remembered something else. Mudhedge raised something up in his hand – his left hand!"

CHAPTER 32

"Don't say a word," Richard Pogue told Theodore Mudhedge. Pogue was a big-time lawyer who had been hired by Reginald Wilson when he had learned about the incident involving his lackey.

"I want time alone with my client," Pogue demanded and Officer O'Malley left the interrogation room. He was signaled back a few minutes later and Captain Davenport joined them in the room.

Davenport confirmed that he had been read his rights and then began questioning Mudhedge. Attorney Pogue wouldn't allow Mudhedge to answer without first whispering to him. The replies came back very vague and uninformative.

"Come on Pogue," the Captain complained. "You are stalling."

"Captain, my client is the victim of a gross misunderstanding. We could walk out of here right now but Mr. Wilson has ordered us to cooperate with the police. Mr. Mudhedge will not be answering any questions but he has told me what happened and if you wish I will relate the story to you before we leave."

"Let's hear it Pogue," the Captain answered with a sigh.

Richard Pogue began by saying that Mudhedge had seen the many social media posts from the three and wanted to follow up with them on a business proposal they had discussed earlier. He arrived at the Rusin garden a little late and then saw the young lady, Ms. Peggy Powell, behind a statue.

Pogue said that Mudhedge was startled but remained friendly and spoke to her and she began acting strangely. She started to move away, tripped and fell. He went to help her but she screamed and then appeared to pass out.

"At that point," Pogue continued, "My client was brutally attacked by a Mr. Dick Jamieson. He was roughly thrown to the ground and restrained and then faced the indignity of being handcuffed by Officer O'Malley. I hope you will be pressing charges against Mr. Jamieson for this violent attack."

"Now, if there is nothing else…" Pogue said as he rose to leave with his client. "Not so fast," the Captain answered. "Ms. Powell indicates that Mr. Mudhedge threatened her with the incendiary phrase 'You don't belong here.'"

"Of course," the attorney answered. Mr. Mudhedge is well aware of the danger of the Cultural Gardens and he was concerned when he saw a young woman all alone there. So he gallantly said, 'You don't belong here.'"

"What about the object he was raising in his left hand?" Pat O'Malley jumped in. Despite Pogue's efforts to keep him quiet, Theodore Mudhedge began explaining. "I pulled out my pocket camera to take a photo of the obviously terrified young lady. As you know, it is the contention of Mr. Wilson and civic minded people everywhere that the Cultural Gardens are a dangerous place and should be made safe."

"Ms. Powell and her two cohorts have been endangering the public with their encouragement to visit the dangerous area. I thought that a photo of one of the three antagonists, obviously terrified to be in the Gardens, might help convince others of the danger and maybe even save some lives."

CHAPTER 33

Pat O'Malley called DJ and recounted the story. "Of course we had to let him go," he said. "Pogue is too good a lawyer. I just hope that they don't go after you for assault. No jury would convict you but it could be a long and expensive hassle."

"How is Peggy feeling?" he continued.

"Physically she is fine," DJ replied but mentally she is messed up. Have you seen the news?"

DJ went on to explain that Reginald Wilson had held an impromptu press conference and was lobbed softball questions by Katrina DeSanto. They had displayed a huge photo of a terrified Peggy cowering behind the bust.

They were pushing the idea that if one of the biggest supporters of the Gardens was in reality terrified to be there it was time for everyone to realize the danger. Peggy was crestfallen. "I blew it guys," she sobbed. "If Wilson's plan goes through and they tear down the Cultural Gardens it will be all my fault."

"No way," Ren replied putting an arm around her. "You didn't do anything wrong. Wilson's crew is crafty. They set you up and our social media postings played right into their hands."

The office phone rang and Dr. Raselok burst out, "How is Peggy?"

"I'm fine Doc," she answered. "Just mortified at my stupidity."

"This has gone too far," the professor went on. "I have let my passion for the Cultural Gardens get in the way of common sense and it almost led to Peggy being harmed. I'm sorry but the project has come to an end."

"But we are so close!" Ren cried. "We just have a few more

gardens to process and we will have them all."

"I'm sorry Ren," replied Dr. Raselok "but if something happens to one of you I won't be able to live with myself."

DJ exchanged glances and nods with the other two and then spoke to their client. "Doc, we have something to tell you. For the last few days we have been secretly working with the police to catch the killer."

"What?" the professor exclaimed. "What do you mean?"

DJ laid out the fourth prong of the plan that Captain Davenport had reluctantly suggested. "It was clear to the Captain, and to us, that the killer was using our social media postings to pick a place for the murders. He, or she, was actually using our social media reach as a way to attract publicity to the crimes."

"Captain Davenport asked us if we would be willing to be guinea pigs to try and lure the killer out. He told us to blast our accounts with our locations and plans and try to get as many hits as possible."

"Guinea pigs!" Raselok interjected, "That's unfathomable. How could a man of law enforcement put you in such danger?

"The Captain promised that they would have undercover officers in the gardens that we had announced we would be covering. Even we don't know who they are. We had a lot of followers today. And Officer O'Malley has been tracking our movements keeping his squad car just far enough away so as not to scare away the killer."

"But Peggy could have been killed – so much for the plan." The professor stated.

"The plan was fine Professor," Peggy sniffled. "But I didn't follow it and the undercover security had already moved on to the next garden to scope it out. It's all my fault."

"Don't blame yourself Peggy," Ren soothed. "We will know better tomorrow."

"Tomorrow? No way," said Dr. Raselok.

"Please Doc," DJ begged. "We are just about done with the project, we will be very careful, there are undercover cops watching over us… We need to do this to save the Cultural Gardens. If we don't show up anymore Wilson and the media will claim that even the Gardens' three biggest fans are afraid to visit and that will be the final nail in the Garden's coffin."

There was a long silence on the line. "I see what you are saying but it is so dangerous. Are you sure you are willing to carry this through?" Dr. Raselok asked.

"Yes, Doc. It should all be over in a few days. Tomorrow we are going to finish up with the Slovak and Greek Gardens. We will continue our social media barrage and maybe the murderer will show himself knowing that the project is winding down. If not, we have the final plan ready."

After letting Dr. Raselok in on the rest of the plan the professor reluctantly agreed to continue. They schedule a meeting to discuss some final project ideas in the Coffee Shop the day after tomorrow. He had made them promise to be extra careful and Peggy assured him she would not stray from the plan again.

The trio bombarded their social media with their plans for the next day. When they arrived at the Slovak Garden they were greeted by a sizeable group of followers. The onlookers made it harder to work because they kept getting in the photos and videos but the three pressed on.

The Slovak Cultural Garden was initially dedicated in 1932 and is comprised of three acres, spanning both levels of the Gardens. Outside of the greenery the main attraction was a sandstone terrace that opens onto an oval-shaped lawn where numerous performances have been held.

There are busts of famous Slovak community leaders Stefan Furdek and Jan Kollar. Furdek served as priest in Cleveland's Our Lady of Lourdes Catholic Church. He organized the First Catholic Slovak Union and the First Slovak Ladies Union in 1889. He was also a prolific author and wrote an important reader that was used widely in Slovakian schools.

Kollar was a Lutheran minister who defended the language rights of both Lutheran and Catholic Slovaks against the encroachment of the Austro-Hungarian Empire. His poetry predicted Slovakian independence.

Between the 2 busts is a huge statue of Slovak hero General Milan R. Stefanik. After a group photo and lots of selfies in front of the Stefanik statue the three led their growing entourage to the Greek Garden.

The Greek Garden was dedicated in 1940. It is a sunken garden following the lines of a Greek cross. The entrance is guarded by two Doric columns which are replicas of those at the Parthenon on the

Acropolis in Athens.

Near the back of the Garden is a reflecting pool in front of a wall in the spirit of the Parthenon, dedicated to the Greek spirit in philosophy, art, literature, and science. The wall is inscribed with the names such as Solon, Euripides, Sophocles, Aeschylus, Homer, Sappho, Socrates, Aristotle, Plato, Demosthenes, Archimedes, Euclid, Hippocrates, Ptolemy, Pythagoras and others.

As the three finished their work, the day took on a party atmosphere. Someone had called a Greek food truck and it was gyros for lunch. Opa!

There were dozens of hangers on and DJ wondered if one of them was the murderer. As the crowd finished the baklava dessert and the food truck pulled away Peggy said that DJ should say something.

Reluctantly, DJ climbed a few steps and said, "Can I have your attention?"

The crowd quieted and DJ thanked them for their support over the last few days. He congratulated them for not being afraid to be in the Cultural Gardens and that he hoped to see them all back on One World Day.

"This place of peace and diversity belongs to all of us – the people of Cleveland – and is a model for the rest of the world. Never let someone take them from us."

Ren tousled DJ's hair, Peggy hugged him and a cheer erupted. The crowd soon dispersed and the three gathered their gear and headed for the studio. "Now the dangerous part begins," a suddenly somber DJ said.

CHAPTER 34

They checked in with Officer O'Malley who said they had not noticed any suspicious activity in the crowd or surrounding gardens all day. O'Malley asked if they were still a go for the final phase of the plan tomorrow and they said they were.

After processing the day's content the three got to work on their social media accounts. They thanked their followers and told how the data collection part of the project was just about done. More information on the completion date of the final book/DVD would be available at their table at One World Day.

They were only slightly surprised at the almost immediate barrage of comments from what had to be a concerted effort by Wilson's minions.

The replies all warned people how dangerous the Gardens were, reminded people how even Peggy had been petrified to be there and cautioned them against attending One World Day. Poor Peggy's fearful photo had become a meme.

Next, the three posted how they had just a few catch up shots to take care of the next morning. They let the world know that they would be splitting up so they could finish fast: Peggy in the Albanian Garden, Ren in the Serbian Garden and DJ in the lower level of the Lithuanian Garden.

They headed downtown for some dinner at another one of their favorite restaurants, Bo Loong. All 3 just picked at their food, delicious as it was. Bo Loong was part of an ever growing AsiaTown neighborhood in Cleveland spanning the East 20's through 40's and bounded by St Clair to Payne Ave.

They loaded their take home Styrofoam containers with the unfinished food. "We have to meet Doc Raselok in the Coffee Shop at 8 AM," DJ reminded them. "So we should probably get some sleep. This will all be over soon."

Silently, DJ worried that it might end in a way they were not expecting. He put the leftovers in the refrigerator and turned in for what turned out to be another fitful night.

The three arrived about the same time the next day at the Cultural Gardens Coffee Shop and found that Dr. Raselok was already there. "What will you have? I started a tab," he offered. After ordering 2 coffees, a "Peggy" and several blueberry muffins they got down to business.

They spent about an hour discussing details of the project – formats, marketing plans, website details and so on. They were starting to get excited. This was not only a big first project for their new company but all 4 were passionate about the Gardens.

Their excitement tempered when Peggy brought up the elephant in the room. "This may be the only way that the Cultural Gardens will be remembered if Wilson gets his way. It will be like photos of the last example of an endangered species in the jungle taken before they went extinct."

Ren grabbed for another muffin and said, "If that happens our project will be even more valuable. It will be like having a complete archive of a destroyed ancient ruin. We'll make a mint!"

Peggy slapped his hand disapprovingly and spilled some of his coffee onto their client. She apologized and grabbed a stack of napkins and started blotting him. "Don't worry Peggy," the prof said, "I got it." He proceeded to sop up the spill and put the rest of the napkins in his pocket.

"While Ren is certainly correct that the project would be exponentially more valuable should the Gardens be destroyed none of us did this for the money anyway, right?" Raselok said and the three nodded in agreement.

"I didn't mean to sound like I wanted that to happen," Ren backtracked. "You know that. I was just looking for a silver lining. Frankly, I am scared."

"Speaking of that," the professor continued, "Even with

undercover police protection wasn't it dangerous to tell the world that you would be splitting up this morning and be in different gardens all alone? I am worried about your safety."

DJ leaned forward and in a low voice said, "That's the final part of the plan, Doc."

He looked around and whispered, "Captain Davenport told us to lure the killer to one of the Gardens where we will supposedly be working all alone. In reality, there will be undercover officers there dressed to look like us. Plus backups in the neighboring gardens."

"I hope my double is as handsome as I am," Ren joked. "We don't need to redo any shots from those gardens. The three of us will be somewhere else."

Working on his 3rd muffin Ren continued, "We still need a few shots up here in the American Garden and the Peace Garden of the Nations. Everybody always forgets those two."

The Peace Garden was right next to the coffee shop. It was dedicated as the American Legion Garden in the 1930's. One of the most interesting parts of the garden, and of any of the gardens actually, is a crypt buried beneath the Peace Monument in the garden.

The crypt contains soil from all over the world. Whenever a new Garden is dedicated a little bit of soil from that country is added to the crypt in a ceremony.

The symbolism is that soil from all these different peoples and countries can coexist in one spot. Inscribed on the monument are these words: "In America, peace, understanding, amity, and cooperation among peoples of all nations."

The three didn't know if they would be able to access the crypt but they really wanted it for the project. They had brought two shovels with them and DJ and Ren were going to give it their best shot.

"Meanwhile I will hop over to the American Garden and reshoot a couple of busts. There are some reflections in our first shots," Peggy added. "And then we can have a celebratory lunch somewhere. I have a craving for Mexican."

The American Garden is spread out from East Blvd and the Irish Garden to the Syrian Garden. It's mostly hilly with a few flat spaces. The bust of Booker T Washington near a flagpole would be Peggy's first stop.

Next would be the bust of Mark Twain. It was far back from the street in an isolated area of the Garden. Students from the nearby school had "adopted" the American Garden in 2009. They work in the garden, raise funds and craft plans for its future.

The foursome had been so intent on sharing their plans that they were startled when Carl and Ernie stopped at their table for some morning banter. "Look at these young people," Ernie teased. "Taking a coffee break before they even did any work." "That's the youth of today," Carl chimed in. "Want their muffins before they even lift a finger."

As they looked up at Carl and Ernie, the group saw other familiar faces in a back corner of the coffee shop. Katrina DeSanto and Theodore Mudhedge were sitting at a table not 10 feet from them.

"Uh oh," Ren worried. "When did they get here? And what did they hear?"

"This could ruin everything," DJ said. "If DeSanto overheard us and posts our plan, our last chance to save the Gardens is ruined."

"Well, well, well. If it isn't the Terrible Trio," Katrina DeSanto said as she approached their table. Aren't you three supposed to be working in the gardens by now? That's what your social media postings say."

"We are on our way, Katrina. Don't worry," Peggy replied.

"By the way," the reporter continued. "You can be the first to know that I will be accepting a position with Mr. Wilson's company. I will be in charge of their PR and press relations. My first task will be letting the world know how Mr. Wilson saved the citizens of Cleveland from a murderer and all this wasted space by taking over this dangerous area and making it a profitable business park."

"You have no soul DeSanto," Ren replied.

"Maybe not," she countered, "but I will have enough money to buy as many souls as I want. Ta ta losers."

"Again with the 'Ta ta'," Ren grumbled.

She walked out the front door waving back at the table. "Forget about her," DJ said. "Let's get back to the plan. They went over a few more details and the excitement of soon completing such an important project returned.

Ren pulled out his phone and they arranged themselves for a selfie of the historic moment. He put his right hand in the middle of the table and said "On three… All for one and one for all."

DJ, Peggy and Doctor Raselok added their hands to the pile and held them there as Peggy said she wanted to say something.

While they were posed with joined hands, the waitress brought over the bill and Doc Raselok signed the credit card slip. Peggy was blushing but managed to get a few sentences out. "I want to thank you Dr. Raselok for the opportunity to do something I love and to make such a difference in the world. And I want to thank you two for everything. You are more than friends or colleagues, you are family."

"OK, it's getting deep in here," Ren said but he and DJ were beaming. "One, two, three, break!" and the four hands disconnected and shot into the air. It was going to be a great day.

They had not noticed Theodore Mudhedge slipping out the back door of the coffee shop.

CHAPTER 35

They set up an appointment with Dr. Raselok for the next day and thanked him for the muffins. DJ and Ren turned right as they exited the door and Peggy headed left.

"Hey Pat, anything going on with the undercover operation yet?" DJ said into his phone. "Not yet," Officer O'Malley replied "but we have everything in place. I think this will all be over soon."

DJ and Ren grabbed their gear, including the two shovels, and approached the Peace Garden. They didn't want to do any damage but they really wanted a shot inside that crypt.

Meanwhile, Peggy started documenting the Booker T. Washington bust. Washington had been born into slavery but became a voice for former slaves and their descendants. He was a key proponent of African-American businesses and one of the founders of the National Negro Business League.

While she was working, Peggy thought she saw the figure of Theodore Mudhedge lurking behind some trees across the street. She was still embarrassed by her earlier fainting episode so there was no way she was going to call the guys.

She grabbed her gear and headed toward the bust of Samuel Clemens, better known as Mark Twain. The bust was situated far back from the street and in a secluded area. She was a little nervous about going back there alone but she took a drink of her "Peggy" for courage and marched on.

Meanwhile, DJ and Ren rested on their shovels and took a break. The crypt was harder to get open than they had expected. "Let's check in with Peggy," DJ said. "No way," Ren replied. "She will be so mad if she thinks we are checking up on her. She'll call us if she needs us. Nobody knows we are here so we are all safe."

"OK," DJ agreed reluctantly. "But if we don't hear from her in 30 minutes I am going to call."

Peggy set her backpack down and started assembling the tripod. She thought about calling DJ and Ren and "checking in" but she knew how that would look. It wasn't worth the inevitable teasing.

Soon she relaxed and got into her work. Twain was a favorite of hers. Most people said that Tom Sawyer or The Adventures of Huckleberry Finn were their favorite Mark Twain book but she had always preferred "The Celebrated Jumping Frog of Calaveras County".

This was a favorite bust too. It was a familiar pose of Mark Twain and, oh, that famous moustache. Sculptor Frank Jirouch created the bust in 1935. At some point over the years the bust went missing but schoolchildren from the nearby school located the missing bust and restored it in 2012.

Peggy circled the bust, capturing every side and angle. DJ and Ren had shared their vast knowledge of photography and videography with her and she was grateful.

Along with the click of the camera's shutter she thought she heard a rustling in the foliage to the side. Mudhedge? Could it be Theodore Mudhedge she worried to herself?

"Get a hold of yourself Peggy," she said and forced herself to turn back to the Twain bust. When she did, she was startled to see a figure emerging from behind the bust.

CHAPTER 36

DJ and Ren finally got the crypt open and shot several frames of video. In reality it was a letdown – just a bunch of dirt. But they knew that it was an historic and important part of the Gardens so they were glad to have documented it.

They had both been in attendance when the last two communities to share soil – the Albanians and Croatians – ceremoniously deposited soil from overseas to the crypt. DJ and Ren were excited at the interest in so many communities in stabling their own cultural garden. They discussed when there might be another soil ceremony with samples from Mexico, Uzbekistan, Egypt, Colombia, France and other new gardens added to the crypt. "Plus, we still don't have soil from Lebanon, Pakistan, Vietnam, Russia, Korea, Turkey and some of the other newer or in progress gardens," DJ added.

They mopped their brows and sat down. "Can you believe Katrina DeSanto and that weasel Mudhedge were in the Coffee Shop this morning?" Ren asked. For two people who seem to hate the Gardens they sure spend a lot of time here."

"I know," DJ added. "I'd feel a lot better if those two would stay far away from the Gardens, and us, at least until the murderer is caught."

"But what if one of them is the murderer?" Ren asked. They started listing the possible killers and what clues they had.

"There are a few people who really benefit from the elimination of the Gardens." DJ stated. "Reginald Wilson of course. Theodore Mudhedge and Katrina DeSanto too. They all come out smelling like a rose if fear causes the city to sell the gardens. But is that enough to kill for? Does anyone else benefit?"

"We don't know much about the murderer from the forensic reports either," Ren added. "Just that he, or she, is a leftie. We know both Mudhedge and DeSanto are left-handed but that's not enough evidence. Lots of people are lefties."

"Well hopefully the undercover sting will work and the killer will be arrested and we can get to work getting ready for One World Day," DJ said.

They sat there thinking when DJ suddenly jerked up. "Oh my God! Peggy!"

CHAPTER 37

"Oh, it's you," Peggy said a little sheepishly. "I thought I saw Theodore Mudhedge lurking around. He scares me."

"No, just me," came the reply. Suddenly a hand covered her mouth and she could not scream. Her arms were held behind her back and she was dragged into the bushes behind the bust.

She was thrust to the ground and her assailant pulled out something from a pocket. It was a napkin from the Cultural Gardens Coffee Shop and Peggy could see that the words "You don't belong here" had already been printed on it.

Terrified, Peggy was unable to scream. She forced herself not to faint knowing that if she did she would never wake up. She struggled as she saw her assailant's left hand holding a rock.

"But Dr. Raselok," she managed to gasp. "Why?"

CHAPTER 38

"Peggy!" DJ shouted as he jumped up and started running toward the American Garden. "We have to get to Peggy. Try getting her on her cell and then follow me. Peggy is in danger!"

Peggy didn't answer Ren's call. Ren had no clue what DJ had figured out but started running after him anyway.

They searched the garden by the Washington and Twain busts but did not see Peggy. They threw down the shovels they had been carrying and began a search.

They spotted Theodore Mudhedge crossing the street. Ren shouted, "I got him Deej." Ren took off after the man and using his martial arts skills had him subdued in seconds. Ren looked around for DJ who was nowhere in sight and assumed he went looking for Peggy.

"Where's Peggy?" Ren shouted at the prone figure. "What have you done with her?"

"Nothing. I didn't do anything to her," Mudhedge cried. Ren placed a foot on his chest and got Mudhedge to admit that he had been following them this morning after seeing them in the coffee shop. He claimed he was just curious as to what they were up to. He too had seen their social media postings and knew they were not supposed to be in this part of the Gardens.

"We'll see what Officer O'Malley has to say about this," Ren threatened. "You're coming with me." Ren held the suspect's arms behind him and marched him back across the street to the area where the Mark Twain bust was.

DJ had gone deeper in the woods looking for Peggy and calling her name. He headed toward the sound of some rustling in the bushes and felt something pressed into his back.

"Don't do anything stupid and put your hands up," a familiar voice said.

"Turn around, slowly," Dr. Trebor Raselok ordered DJ. "And don't make a sound or Peggy gets it first and then you."

DJ did as he was told and saw an ashen faced Peggy sitting on the ground looking terrified. DJ asked her with his eyes if she was OK and she managed to nod and mouth the word "yes."

"Where is the third Musketeer?" Raselok sneered. "Ren is on his way to the police. He knows that you are the murderer and is telling them everything. You won't get away with it Doc," DJ said.

"Nice try Mr. Jamieson," the prof replied. "But there is no way he or anyone could have figured out it was me. He is probably off following Mudhedge. I saw him lurking around. And by the time he realizes that it isn't him I will be long gone and I'm afraid, so will you two."

Raselok ordered DJ to sit down next to Peggy. DJ put his arm around his friend and held her protectively. Peggy seemed to gather some strength from the hug and managed to whisper "Why?" to their former client.

"Why? Don't be naïve little girl. Why? I'll tell you why," the professor responded. "I am a genuine fan of the Cultural Gardens and all they stand for. That's why I hired you three to help document them and make them known to the world. But I am also a realist. It became apparent that even though this was going to be a quality product on a unique and special topic it would only reach a few hundred or maybe thousand people. That was frustrating."

"But then," he continued, "there was a murder. Suddenly the Cultural Gardens and my project were making national and international news. The reach of the finished product instantly went from hundreds to thousands. But I realized that the interest would soon fade unless…"

"Unless there were more murders," DJ chimed in.

"Yes, Mr. Jamieson. I could not have asked for a more delicious and media friendly component of the crime as that note on the napkin. 'You don't belong here' became a trending topic on social media and I knew it had to continue."

"You were so clueless," the professor continued. "It was easy to capitalize on your social media because you posted all your locations and activities. I made sure to continue the interest by acting in gardens that you had been publicizing. Katrina DeSanto played right into my hand. And I couldn't have even anticipated my good fortune when Reginald Wilson started his campaign. Every time there was a murder the number of projected sales grew exponentially."

"You are insane," DJ murmured. "You won't get away with it."

"Oh, but I will," Raselok responded ominously. "All your content is on our shared server in the cloud so I will have access to it." Raselok explained. "Your colleague Mr. Wu will work his magic as a memorial to you two and we will create a blockbuster product. The untimely death of 2 of the 3 authors will guarantee this is an international best seller. My beloved Gardens will be captured for eternity and my bank balance will have several zeroes added to it."

"Two problems Doc," DJ countered. "If I was able to figure out it was you, Ren or Officer O'Malley or Captain Davenport or someone else will too."

"Yes, Mr. Jamieson. That does interest me," Raselok said, "Explain to me why you suspected me?"

"It was easy," DJ explained. "We knew two things about the murderer; that he had to benefit from the killings in some way and that he was left-handed. We could pretty much eliminate the other people who would clearly benefit like Wilson, Mudhedge and DeSanto, and never really considered Ernie or Carl or any of the Garden Federation reps."

"When we were toasting the project in the coffee shop we all had our hands – our right hands – joined in the middle. You managed to sign the credit card slip with your left hand. It didn't click till later but when I was wondering who else might benefit from the murders I remembered that you were a leftie too."

"Well done, Mr. Jamieson," Raselok said. "Too bad nobody else will put that together. You said there was another issue?"

DJ took a breath and said "All the killings were done with a blunt object striking the head by a left hand. You have a gun now. That will be easy to trace and someone will hear the shots. You won't get away with it."

"Ah, but I will," Raselok grinned.

CHAPTER 39

"Here is how this will work. I am going to strike you on the head with this rock." Raselok pointed to a softball size rock at his feet. "And you will allow it. Don't worry, it will be over within a second, virtually painless."

"Why would I do that?" DJ asked. "You really are insane if you think I will let you kill me without a fight."

"I think you will Mr. Jamieson," Raselok said as if he was explaining something in front of a classroom. "This can be an easy process or a very painful process. If you make it easy for me, I will make it easy on your friend. One quick blow to the head. She won't suffer at all. But if you give me a hard time, I will make sure that she suffers immensely before her demise. It's your call."

Peggy looked at DJ. "Don't," she begged. "Don't cooperate. I will be OK. Let's fight him together. Don't make it easy on him."

DJ smiled at his friend and said "Don't worry Peggy. It will all be over soon. I am not going to let him make you suffer."

He kissed her on the forehead, gave her a squeeze and stood up. "Let's get this over with Raselok," he growled. "And if you break your promise and make Peggy suffer I will haunt you for eternity."

DJ had no intention of letting Raselok just hit him in the head and kill him but he hadn't come up with a plan yet. He knew he had to stall until Ren or someone found them.

Likewise, Peggy was prepared to do whatever she had to do from preventing Raselok from killing DJ. Would screaming help? Could she make a grab for the gun? Her mind raced.

DJ thought that if this was going to be the end he would at least do what he could to make it hard for Raselok. He was going to make him fire that gun. At least someone might hear the shot or at least it would be more clues for the police.

His heart sank as he saw Raselok screwing something onto the end of his gun. DJ had seen enough TV to know that it was a silencer. So much for someone hearing the shots.

Suddenly DJ saw Ren coming through the bushes with Mudhedge in tow. Raselok swung the gun toward Ren and Mudhedge and the professor said "How fortuitous. I now will have all 3 of the little garden heroes murdered and their killer, Mr. Mudhedge, will take his own life in a final act of remorse."

Ren and Mudhedge stared at the scene with their mouths open. What was going on? Why did Doc Raselok have a gun pointed at them?

Raselok turned and pointed the gun back at DJ's head and cocked it. The little clearing echoed with a loud "Thwack, Thwack."

CHAPTER 40

DJ braced at the noise. He was surprised that he didn't even feel the gunshots. He opened his eyes and saw Carl and Ernie holding shovels – the shovels that he and Ren had dropped as they ran to save Peggy.

They were grinning and both had a foot on Raselok who was lying on the ground looking confused and in obvious pain. Ren looked even more confused but soon was jumping up and down while hugging Peggy who was both laughing and crying. Mudhedge looked like he was in the Twilight Zone.

Office Pat O'Malley, Captain Davenport and 3 undercover officers came sprinting up to the group and took in the scene.

"What the heck have you three done now?" the Captain moaned. "Is that Dr. Raselok on the ground? Is he OK? Was he attacked?"

Everyone started talking at once until the Captain raised his hands and said, "One at a time!"

"He's the attacker," Ernie answered "and my brother in arms – well, shovels - and me took him down. We saw the kids at the coffee shop this morning and on our way back to our gardens we saw the shovels they had left in the American Garden."

"We were going to chew them out for leaving the garden a mess," Carl continued, "when we heard some commotion further into the woods."

"As we got closer, we saw this guy," Ernie pointed at Raselok, "pointing a gun at DJ's head. So we took up our trusty shovels and 'thwack, thwack' knocked him down."

The officers couldn't help but smile and soon everyone was slapping the heroes on the back and shaking hands. Even Mudhedge seemed relieved.

"We're going to need you both to come down to the station and make an official statement," ordered Captain Davenport who was regaining his 'official' demeanor. "Anything else either of you would like to add in the meantime?"

"Never mess with a veteran," Carl replied as Ernie nodded and the pair shared a warm high five.

EPILOGUE

DJ, Ren and Peggy were exhausted. It was the day after One World Day in the Cleveland Cultural Gardens. The annual event had attracted record crowds this year, partly because of all the recent publicity.

One World Day had gone off without incident. Tens of thousands had enjoyed the day sharing and learning about the diverse cultures of their neighbors. The music, dancing, performances and, of course, food made it one of the best One World Day's in memory – even Ernie's long memory.

They had sold hundreds of advanced orders for their book/DVD project and their email showed hundreds of other online orders.

A contribution jar on their table had collected enough funds to give Angel Annie a proper burial.

Paul, Lex, Tom, Joyce, Gia Hoa and all the other Cultural Gardens volunteers were busy cleaning up after One World Day and planning their next projects. Just as it should be.

Ernie and Carl had become folk heroes. The two different but similar people had saved the day and maybe the Cultural Gardens. Their story was told and retold as an example of how we may seem different but actually have much more in common than we may think. A perfect takeaway from the Cultural Gardens.

After Raselok's evil scheme had been revealed, the public and political support for Reginald Wilson's plan had eroded. He and Mudhedge and his new PR Captain Katrina DeSanto were forced to move on to other projects and leave the Cultural Gardens alone. They never did hold their rally.

Katrina DeSanto tried to get her Cleveland Press job back but her journalistic credibility had been shattered.

DJ, Ren and Peggy had seen their social media presence grow exponentially. Their startup company was receiving lots of attention and requests to bid. It looked like they just might be able to build a sustainable company doing the work they loved.

But that was for another day. Right now, the three put their feet up, dug into dinner and prepared for some mindless binge watching.

After a few minutes of discussion on what to watch, Ren shouted "I've got it. Let's watch the Mod Squad!" They all laughed and Ren cued up Season 1 Episode 1.

He was about to hit Play when the office phone rang. The caller ID showed Captain Davenport. DJ sighed and looked at his friends before pressing the speaker button.

"Glad I caught you," the Captain said. "Can you be in my office at 8AM tomorrow?"

"Now what? Did we do something wrong?" Ren moaned with his finger still over the Play button.

"No, I need your help." the Captain answered, "There's been a murder in AsiaTown."

THE END

AUTHOR'S NOTE

The setting for this book is a real place. The Cleveland Cultural Gardens are 254 acres of land mostly on East and MLK Boulevards in Cleveland, Ohio. The land was donated by John D. Rockefeller and the first garden was established in 1917.

Much of the description of the actual gardens is accurate but some literary license had been employed. Visit the official website of the Cleveland Cultural Gardens at www.clevelandculturalgardens.org for accurate and current descriptions. Some of the characters are based on real people but again, this is a work of fiction and it is not intended to depict any person living or dead.

The author has been a fan of the Cleveland Cultural Gardens and all they stand for since he "discovered" them about 15 years ago. He and his sister Debbie and mother Pat capture events and activities in the Gardens for their www.ClevelandPeople.com website which celebrates the 120 or so distinct ethnic groups represented in the Cleveland area.

Dan and Debbie both became members of the board of directors of the Cleveland Cultural Gardens Federation, the non-profit group of volunteers who take care of and grow the gardens.

If you are in the NE Ohio area, the Cleveland Cultural Gardens is a must-visit location. They are unique in the world and tell the story of the people who came to Cleveland and the United States from all over the world and live together in peace through mutual understanding.

Visit www.MurderintheCulturalGardens.com for more information and a preview of the next book in the series featuring DJ, Ren and Peggy called Murder in AsiaTown.

Made in the USA
Middletown, DE
13 May 2021